A Very Bennett Christmas:

A Diary of Murders Novella

by Sarah Cook

For more information, email: sarah@sarahcookwriter.co.uk

First paperback edition November 2024

Edited by Steven Cook
Cover design by Sarah Cook

978-1-7393470-9-3 – Paperback

www.sarahcookwriter.co.uk

For the ghosts of past, present, and future

CONTENT WARNING:

Dearest Reader,

Please enjoy this racy Christmas story but be mindful that it contains detailed depictions of sex.

This includes BDSM, femme-domme and male-sub dynamics, riding crops, ejaculation play, and group sex (MFFM).

There are also references to child abuse and neglect.

This particular novella has a HFN ending.

Thank you,

Sarah Cook

Chapter One:

The Morning

Wednesday 25th December 1895

The Bennetts were asleep, to begin with…

The day was barely awake itself. The light of the morning stayed barred by the grey clouds that covered the sky. The sun still yawning behind the bleariness. The streets of London had not yet erupted into its usual chatter and were equally as dormant as the two doctors. Though there was a hue of excitement in the air, the cheeriness was kept within closed doors, nestled by freshly stoked fireplaces and carefully wrapped presents. The magic of the day was the only thing truly alive: that and the wind as it howled across the cobbles and through the alleyways.

At eight o'clock in the morning, the Bennetts were enjoying what they perceived to be a well-earned lie-in. They lay as they did most mornings with John on his back and Miriam snuggled on his chest as he lazily dangled an arm over her shoulder. Both nude, wrapped up in sheets and one another, their bedroom was all but silent – save for the low timbre of Miriam's snores.

A particularly loud one rumbled throughout the quiet causing John to jolt awake. His sudden jump made Miriam to groan and nestle further into him. With his eyes still closed, he chuckled slightly as her breathing deepened and she fell back asleep. There was a part of him that wished to join her in that peaceful slumber, but his heart was now racing. The beat thudded against his chest making him blissfully aware of how alive he was. Fluttering his eyes; he stayed there, valuing the stillness of the room and inhaling intensely to calm his pulse down.

Suddenly a realisation gripped him with an insurmountable giddiness which made his eyes snap fully open. A broad grin stretched across his face. Today was the 25th of December – Christmas Day. A truly magical day indeed. One would suspect that at thirty-nine, Doctor John Bennett would've dispensed with all notions of childlike glee surrounding Christmas, but the opposite was in fact true. For John, this was to be the first Christmas of the rest of his life. The first Christmas where he was truly happy. The first Christmas with his wife – Miriam.

Until this very moment, Christmas had different connotations for him. As a child, his family was poor, and his parents worked through most of the holidays. However, they still had their traditions. His parents instilled in him that generosity still came in small packages. Every year they often surprised him with a well-cooked chicken feast and a meagre but meaningful gift such as a chocolate bar or chalk. His favourite part, however, was the evening when they would light a red candle and watch it burn just a little bit to signal the closing of the year, praying their thanks for still being alive and still being here. They would save the candle for the next Christmas.

When his father died, his mother carried on the tradition even though it was harder without your soulmate. Then his mother too passed away, and John was carted off to his awful Aunt Evelyn. Christmas stopped being magical and became more gruelling. His aunt would force him to read the bible and attend church to atone for being a wicked child. His Christmas dinner became merely soup and a roll. Yet despite this, when she sent him up to his room, he made sure to light that red candle that he had secreted away. He'd leave it smouldering just a little bit whilst he would pray for the souls of his mother and father. But he couldn't quite be thankful that he was still alive.

That candle was a stub now with not much life left in the wick. After he left the clutches of his aunt, he carried on the tradition into adulthood. His Christmases were almost entirely alone. He'd read a good book, have a good meal, and help deliver meals to the less well-off men who were blighted by the harsh winter of London. At night, however, he would still light the candle; grateful to be here though his purpose was murky, and he could not help but feel a pang of longing that always came from being alone.

Now as he lay with her nestled in his arms, her breath skimming across his chest, he was like a young boy again, believing in the wonder of the season and all the gifts that it had given him. He couldn't wait to ignite the last remains of the candle and truly show gratitude for how joyous his life had become. A sea of ecstasy waved through him, causing his toes to curl as he gripped tightly onto her body. Unable to stand another second without her, he kissed her on the forehead to gently coax her awake.

As his lips brushed up against her skin, Miriam let out a squeak of approval. She stretched out her legs like a cat unfurling as the sensations skimmed down her. She kept her eyes closed, however, squeezing them shut as though it was abhorrent to even think about opening them. There was nothing quite like staying here in the arms of her husband. The serenity it brought her was unparalleled. She allowed the feeling to wash over her as she listened to his heartbeat intently. There was much to do on this holiest of days, so much that she had planned, but there was nothing quite as important as this very moment.

At twenty-eight, Miriam was still a big fan of Christmas. There was always something quite whimsical about the holiday that made her feel giddy. She adored the groups singing carols on street corners and made sure she stopped to listen to at least one song. She salivated over the wisps of freshly baked apple and cinnamon in the air. She liked the piercing chill as she wrapped up warm in colourful capes and scarves. And whilst she had no poise and balance for it, she really loved watching people ice-skate as the whoosh of blades cut across the ice. There was not a single thing about Christmas that she hated.

The most incredible thing about the holiday, however, was the generosity. Perhaps thanks to Dickens and his miserly fable, the season opened up people in the best kind of way. They showered love on those close to them. There was more appreciation for one's man. People were giving to charities and showed that they cared about the needy. Winter could be especially cruel to the poor and many provided food and shelter for those in lesser circumstances. Miriam often wished to make that spirit stay for the rest of the year. She was determined, in her own ferocious way, to encourage man to be kind every single day, rather than just the one.

She could not wait to share these moments with her husband. The thought of doing so made her snap her eyes open as she stretched her arms and legs again, sneakily wiping the pool of drool from his chest after she had slept on it. John wrapped another arm around her. "Merry Christmas, my darling girl."

"Merry Christmas, my dear husband," she replied with a beaming smile as she turned her gaze upwards. Her pulse leapt into her throat as her eyes caught his bright blue ones. He stared at her in a manner unlike any other. It was as though he could never quite believe that she was here, lying in his arms, completing him entirely. An emotion that she echoed, for she too couldn't quite trust that this was real and not some dream that she was still having. To prove this was their life now and not some fragment of her imagination, she pushed herself off him and leaned over to kiss him deeply. He moaned immediately as her lips crashed into his.

When they parted, upon the crest of a sigh, he uttered, "This is already far better than any Christmas I have had before."

"And yet the day has barely begun!" She fluttered a wink before she leaned over to her bedside cabinet and opened the drawer. She cared not that the top half of her was wild and free, though she kept the sheets draped across both of their waists. After some rummaging, Miriam removed a small rectangular package, tied with a red ribbon, as she spoke in a flurry. "Now, I am aware that I had strict instructions regarding presents, but I saw this in a sordid little shop and could not resist. I thought it would be rather amusing to open this morning."

She spun back around with the gift in her hand and to her surprise, John was sat up. His cheeks began to flush a little though there was a cheeky glint in his eyes and a smile underneath his handlebar moustache, which was slightly askew this morning. She looked down and found in his hands was also a small rectangular parcel wrapped in a green ribbon. When she met his eyes again, he smiled. "I could not resist either."

"Oh you are a terror!"

"As are you!"

They chuckled as they exchanged the gifts and began tearing at the brown paper packaging. Miriam had been quite insistent about the limits on presents for the day. It had become a family tradition. Both Miriam and her father Sir Fredric Clayton felt as though they had enough wealth and trinkets that it was always silly to indulge in more than needed. As Miriam grew older, the number of gifts under the tree dwindled until it became just one each. And it was always exchanged at dinner after they had worked during the day. When she had married John, Miriam had opened up a little bit more to accommodate him: One for all at Christmas dinner, and one exchanged between the pair later that evening. It was better that way. After all, their presents to one another were always so salacious.

Even this morning's little treat was too cheeky to be seen by any other family member. In almost unison, they opened their parcels and immediately burst into huge whoops of laughter. They had gotten one another the same gift. A little book of rude words and vulgarities. Miriam had found hers in a pokey bookshop in Brick Lane, nestled in the darkest corners of the shelves. It shocked the keeper to see a woman buying such a book, especially as she giggled and tittered whilst he wrapped it up for her.

"My, what a coincidence," John said as he flipped the cover. He did not have to travel very far. Instead, he had wandered into his favourite crooked yet quaint bookstore in Soho and found it amongst the saucier stories. The shop owner expressed equal confusion at seeing the usually reserved and quiet doctor buy such a titillating title.

"Indeed, it seems we are truly perfectly matched." Miriam grinned proudly before she leaned over and kissed him again. She then peeled open her version of the book and started merrily flipping through the pages. "Let us find the best ones."

John nodded and mirrored her action. He was the first to find a comical term. "Good Heavens! 'Dugs'."

"'Dugs?"

He gestured to her big breasts as they dangled down her chest. "'Dugs'."

"No," she gasped as she hid her bosom playfully with one arm. "Oh… no… I do not like that one bit. That is awful."

"There's also 'diddies'?" he replied with a raise of his eyebrow. She shook her head at him. He then flicked through a couple of pages. "What about 'ripe fruits'? Hmmm no. Not sure if I am too keen on that one. Oh, ha ha, here is an absolutely cracking term. 'Ruby-tipped globes'."

"That is a mouthful."

"They certainly are." He turned downward to his wife's bountiful display. He immediately and so urgently wanted to dive in – roll his tongue across the curves, kiss the trail between them, and even take a nipple between his teeth. He felt a slight stiffening at the very thought of nestling in his wife's skin.

Miriam shoved him playfully. She turned back to the book. "Here are a few that I like; 'Lobcock'?"

"I have actually heard that one before. It means flaccid penis, does it not?"

"Very good."

"I have no such problem now."

Miriam looked down at his crotch as John reached down to grab it. She could see the outline of his hard generous member against the white cotton fabric. She bit onto her lip to stop herself from throwing the book across the room and climbing on top. A heated sensation crept between her legs, and she squeezed her thighs together. She turned her sights back to her husband's face and caught a cheeky glint in his eyes as one side of his mouth curled into a smile. A hot heated breath scurried out of her nose. "I find it truly remarkable that anyone would dare think of you as shy, my utterly wanton man."

He kissed her on the shoulder. "Only for you my dark goddess."

"So I guess you would prefer 'prodigious engine'?"

"Oh yes." He placed his copy on the side as he shuffled closer against her. His hand started to play with strands of her mousey-brown hair. "Oh yes, I like that a lot."

Miriam kept flicking through hers. She wanted to tease him, knowing that he was hankering for her body in the same way she was almost desperate for his. She studiously ignored his advances. "I quite like this one..." She snorted as she kept her eyes fixed on the page. "'Cloven inlet.' It means a woman's privates."

"Cloven inlet?" John frowned.

"Yes, I suppose because, well, for some women it looks like a cloven foot." She felt herself getting hot as she tried to explain to her husband. Especially when she met eyes, and they immediately darkened. She couldn't help but think on all the naked women she had seen. Their bodies were always so powerful and beautiful.

She tried not to grin too much as she remembered being buried in some. She was wet already but now she was achingly so.

"Hmmm, I cannot picture it." John's eyes darted over her face, almost as if he could see the flickering sapphic images in her mind. He skimmed his tongue across his bottom lip as he dropped his voice to a low rumble. "Perhaps you could show me?"

Miriam giggled. "Very well."

She threw the sheets from her body and revealed her whole self to him. She kept one hand clutching onto the book whilst she dragged the other down her body. She nestled her fingertips in her pubic hair, pushing it apart softly to show her husband. John eyed her face for a little while before he slowly travelled down her nude body. A small groan of appreciation left his lips when he saw her glistening wet vagina. He uttered breathily, "I see."

"Show me your…" Miriam turned back to the book. "'White-staff' please John."

He nodded, pushing the remaining blankets from his person. She studiously watched him as, now free from the cloth confines, his prick stood to attention. John had never disliked his body. He had a tall, thin frame, muscles from his partiality for sport, a small stomach from a plentiful appetite, and beds of thick black hair across his body. Yet when Miriam looked at him, as though she had just unearthed the greatest treasure, he felt more alive and more confident in himself. Her tongue slipped out of her lips and her teeth nestled onto the bed as though she were keeping her wants guarded. "What do you wish me to do?" he whispered.

"As always, I wish for you to kneel."

He scrambled quickly to his knees so that he and his erection loomed over her. An electric charge shot through her. He was so easy to command. "Good boy." Smiling, she focused instead on her book. She wasn't really reading, but she bobbed her head as though she were. Her fingers were still nestled in her wetness - frozen as she kept John in suspense as to what her next instruction could be. His breaths shallowed in anticipation as he shuffled on his knees. "John, take your 'truncheon' and start 'fetching mettle' for me." Darting her eyes over, she clocked his confused expression. "Touch yourself. Slowly. Very slowly."

Miriam snapped the book shut causing him to jump. He nodded and cupped his hand across his stiff member. He did as instructed, stroking himself unhurriedly as twinges already began to travel down his staff. Miriam watched for a little bit before she placed her book on the dresser. She kept her eyes locked upon his as she wriggled slightly down and began moving her fingers. John gulped a little as his hand gradually stroked himself.

She gasped as her fingers dived through her folds. She coated the tips of them with her own lubrication before she settled on her clitoris. Sighing, she said eagerly, "Now, move a little bit faster John but you must not climax until I tell you so, do you understand?"

"I understand." John did as he was instructed, moving at a more giving pace, pushing and pulling his hand upon his dick. Small sounds escaped his mouth as he did.

"Very good," she moaned as her fingertips circled her sensitive spot, she kept her sights fixated on him. The way his thick member was hard and throbbing for her was an unforgettable sight to behold. She thought about the way it felt inside of her and suddenly her fingers grew faster, rubbing herself with an unparalleled need.

Without instruction, however, John fiddled quicker still. All because he cherished seeing her masturbate so giddily. Miriam was beautiful. Her large, teardrop breasts jiggled as her body thrust against her hand. Her gorgeous plump stomach bounced also as her thick thighs clustered and contracted. She gasped and groaned as her eyes floated between his face and his cock. Her fingers were rapid as she watched him.

He felt like an adonis who could bring this absolute goddess to the height of pleasure merely by being gazed at. He wanted a lot of things: To carry on staring at her beautiful buxom form; to show her just how remarkable she was in a plentiful release; and to be inside of her, completing her in every way.

He let out an unexpected grunt.

He was about to come. He knew it. He couldn't follow her instructions. He couldn't help it. He couldn't hold back.

She must've known it also because suddenly she said, "No John, not yet. Not until I—"

"Oh God," he bellowed before he ejaculated. Semen jetted out of him. Streams of white sticky stuff landed on her plush belly and glorious breasts. He kept his hand pumping his cock until he was completely done coating her. With once last shudder, he had finished. Immediately, he hung his head down low.

Miriam had stopped touching herself and blinked, alarmed at what had happened. There was an uneasiness in the air, one tinged with unknowing. She cocked her head towards him. "I did not give you permission."

"Forgive me." He trembled slightly, partly because he was afraid that he had upset her greatly and partly because he was excited about his punishment. Two hounds of hell raced together within him so fiercely that he was almost certain he was about to harden again.

She dipped her fingers into the silvery pool upon her body. "What an absolute mess you have created."

"I am s—"

"Clean it up," she said sternly, as a teacher would telling off an insolent child.

John nodded before he clambered around the bed and room to see what was nearby. He settled on a discarded shirt on the floor and went to scoop it up.

Miriam grabbed his arm to stop him. "No, John." She inhaled deeply. "I wish for you to use your mouth. Lick it up."

He turned to gawk at her. "What?"

"Lick… it… up." She grinned slyly. "This is your punishment."

John swallowed. Oh, Miriam was a tricky creature indeed. Whenever he thought he had mastered her debauched ideas that she had, she would always surprise him. She was wildly inventive and brewed with such an entrancing dark desire that he found himself meeting her demands. He lay down on the bed and crawled over to her nude body. He hesitated slightly before he slipped out his tongue and ran it across one of the trails on her skin. The taste was salty and bitter as it painted his mouth and slithered down his throat. The act itself was just as provoking as it was shameful, twisting in his stomach with an absolutes splendour.

Miriam watched as John knelt between her legs, giving him a better scope of her nakedness as his tongue trundled over the landscape of her flesh. Whilst he had started slowly, grappling with the naughtiest notion that she had delivered, he grew more confident. He coiled the muscle to scoop up the offending substance from her breasts and swallowed. Such perfect obedience from this willing slave. A swell of sin screwed through her insides, but she tried not to show it. Instead, she watched like stoic royalty.

When he had cleaned up as much as he could, he sneaked up to her and kissed her deeply, slipping his coated tongue into her mouth so she too could have a taste. She murmured and wrapped her arms around his body, bringing him closer to her flesh. The tip of his freshly hardened dick pressed against her heated and moist entrance. He pulled himself away from her lips to ask, "May I?"

Miriam giggled. "No."

He shook his head a little in disbelief. He was ravenous and cloying to be inside of her. He tried again. "Please?"

"No." She placed his hands upon his chest and pushed him slightly upwards from her. There was a twisted light within her eyes that enchanted him. "Not now, anyway."

He fell to one side in exasperation. "But you have yet to climax?"

"I am aware but…" She suddenly clamoured out of bed and reached for her teal dressing gown that had been discarded on a chair nearby. As she placed her arms into the silk fabric, she was acutely aware that he was watching her with an inane look of incredulity. When she tied the garment across her body, she smiled. "… somehow it is more delicious to deny myself, knowing that it would torment you also."

John threw his head back against the pillow and let out a loud irritated heated breath from his nose. She was right, of course. The fact that she had yet to orgasm from their morning tryst was irritating him like a small cut on the roof of his mouth. He tongued at the wound. "You are tricky *Mrs* Bennett." He had forsaken her medical moniker to provoke her.

She winked at him in response before she placed her hands on her hips, "Come now *Mr* Bennett, let us not dally any longer. It is Christmas Day and there are many festivities to be had!"

Chapter Two:

The Drive

The courtyard of The Clayton Hospital was busy.

A line of people snaked within the triangular area. They filled the space the best they could before they extended inside, across the reception area and out of the main entrance. There was a dull chatter which battled against a group of carol singers belting out Good King Wenceslas in one of the corners.

People waited patiently to be served by the volunteers led by Doctor Miriam Bennett.

Every year, on this special day, Miriam would find herself at the hospital taking care of the patients who could not leave due to their illnesses. However, this year, Miriam had decided to organise a charity drive. Not just for those tragic souls left alone in their hospital beds but for poorer people of society. She opened the courtyard to feed them a hearty meal and gift them a care package, filled with warm garments to help with the harsh cold.

The Clayton Hospital was a great place to host a drive such as this. It stood at Piccadilly, near Soho – an area that housed many unfortunates. The hospital itself was a bastion of welfare and care. Created by Sir Fredric Clayton, Miriam's father, it was one of the few places that treated different classes of patients the same and funnelled as much money as possible to keep serving those in need.

It was a much respected hospital where Miriam worked happily as a physician and Head of the Women's Wards. She had met John there only a few months ago when he started working as Deputy Head of Surgery. Their attraction was almost immediate. Their love quick to develop. And their marriage speedily planned when they realised they could not stand being parted for even a second.

Neither paid any mind to the scandal.

He stood, now, proudly beside her in the courtyard, having aided every step of this venture. She had enlisted as many people as she could to help. Her best friend Adelaide Jenkins had spent a handful of weeks knitting scarves and gloves for the care packages. Sir Fredric had spent all of last night and the morning cooking huge vats of soup, gravy, and vegetables as well as several geese before he sent them over. Her aunt Isobel had donated heavily to the cause and helped Miriam shop for small presents that people could open. Even Michael had reached out to his sister Catherine who made tea cakes for each parcel and several apple pies that were sliced as a perfect end for the hearty meal. Miriam and John had spent most of Christmas Eve putting hundreds of packages together.

Helping the Bennetts today were Matron Lockett, and a dark-brown-haired curvy nurse named Barnard. They all stood together, braving the winter's chill to deliver bowls of soup and plates of vegetables, potatoes, and chicken to the needy. Miriam had dressed herself and John in their best Christmas outfits for the occasion as well, in hopes that they would bring cheer to all. She wore a red tartan dress that had a big hoop shirt, and matched it with a similar coloured striped bonnet, velvet deep emerald cape, and scarlet gloves. John wore his black leather coat with fur trim lining, but his trousers and jacket underneath were green tartan with a cherry waistcoat and bow tie. He wore his black top hat and matching brown scarf and gloves to stave off the winter chill.

They had been there for an hour already and had got into an almost factory line-like precision. At first Nurse Barnard would give a warm mug of mulled wine and an empty portable box with four metal bowls inside. Then another nurse would fill one bowl with soup, and another with vegetables. Matron would carve goose slices and drizzle the meat with gravy when asked. John would then slice a piece of pie for the final bowl. Finally, Miriam would give a brown paper package filled with clothing and presents. They efficiently served as many people as possible, all whilst each of them hummed whatever carol the church group were warbling.

When there was a small break in the music, John quipped, "I must say that I am surprised that Adelaide is not here with us."

Adelaide was a great supporter of Miriam's charity ventures. Especially the women's shelter that Miriam was building in her childhood manor in the country. Adelaide was married to the hospital's pharmacist, and John's closest ally, Michael Jenkins, whose relationship with Miriam was often strained. He had archaic views and saw her as a renegade who needed to be curtailed. Still, since the Bennett's wedding in October, the four had grown close. Very close, indeed.

Miriam scoffed. "You know as well as I do that Michael is steadfast in his traditions, particularly when it comes to attending church. I am most certain Adelaide tried her hardest." As she turned around to grab another parcel, she said something under her breath that he couldn't quite catch. It sounded like, "later."

As the choir began again, this time springing into something more melodious, John shook his head with a small chuckle and went back to serving the dessert. He found himself thinking about church. The Bennetts did not subscribe greatly to religion for a multitude of reasons. The last time they were even together in church was their wedding day but that had come at the insistence of her father and her aunt. For Miriam, she could subscribe to the teachings of Christianity and the possibility of a God yet did not believe one should waste their time in futile worship. Surely, as the bible preaches, that time would be best spent helping one's fellow man.

John did, also, have some faith that God existed but that belief was more complex and held a darkness within it. His aunt had wielded religion as though it were a weapon. She used the bible to make him feel powerless and dirty. At ten, he was made to believe that he was a sinful creature who was destined for Hell. She beat him to purify him, using the word of God as an excuse. Worse still were the times when he pleaded for salvation but was met with absolute silence - his prayers abandoned. Since then, his relationship with God had been tricky at best.

Besides, the only church he needed was the altar of his wife's body.

He smiled just thinking of the prayers that she had already answered. His cheeks grew rosy as he sliced into the last remaining pie to distract himself from the titillating ideas. For all at once, he wanted to grab her hand and run up to his office so he could show her the depths of his worship.

It was not long, however, before the queue had dissipated. When they were running low on food and parcels, Miriam stationed another nurse at the door to dissuade anyone else from joining the queue and leaving empty-handed. It did not help ease the stab of guilt she felt for not being able to help everyone who was in desperate need of nourishment and food. On top of this, she was also worried she hadn't seen Marie, a local sex worker, and agonised on how her friend was keeping warm. She tried to choke down the remorse that burned like bile at the back of her throat. Sighing, she counted the number of heads in the courtyard and the parcels. Satisfied that it was an equal number, she exhaled and relaxed her posture.

A young small woman was last to receive her meal. She shuffled down the line politely and quietly. As she did, she let out a small thank you in a dialect that Miriam did not recognise entirely. Miriam was busy with the penultimate man who was shaking her hand profusely, but she did hear a few gasps and even a kindly tut from Matron. When she was freed from the man's grasp, she turned to pick up the last remaining package. However, spinning back around, she nearly dropped it from her hands.

The young woman in question was thin – almost gaunt. Miriam guessed that she was a fair few years younger than herself, perhaps barely scraping twenty. She had scraggly blonde hair underneath a pale blue bonnet. Her clothes were practically rags and covered in dirt. Shivering, she stood with her tray that those before Miriam had piled with all the remains of the dishes. It was then that Miriam clocked what had made Matron let out her sound. Clinging onto the woman's leg was a young girl who must've been merely five, similarly in near-pieces and wrapped up in blankets nestled in the crook of her arm was a small baby fast asleep against her. Both children were similarly bony and shivering from the cold air. Miriam's heart panged in her chest. There was only one package left. She found herself hesitating to hand it over, only because she was worried that it wasn't enough. They needed so much more. So much more than Miriam could give them right now. She was also aware that the procession was all watching her, even though they were busying themselves with tidying up.

As she handed over the package, the woman shook her leg and the young girl ungripped it and reached up for the gift. In an extremely timid voice, the little child said, "Thank you."

Miriam felt helpless as the family turned to walk away. Their tiny weak bodies shuffled out of the courtyard with their measly meal and paltry parcel. Miriam wasn't quite sure what she was about to do when she ran from behind the table and grabbed the woman's shoulder, causing her to turn around. She smiled at the mother before she bent down to put her cape over the girl's shoulders. It was big so most of it covered a lot of the girl's body. Miriam similarly wrapped her scarf around the child. The girl smiled gratefully as she clung onto the fabric. Miriam stood up and placed her gloves carefully on top of the sleeping baby.

But it wasn't enough. Not enough for them all. She had no idea where they were sleeping, no idea if they were safe, no idea what was going to happen to the family when they left the courtyard. She hesitated, unsure what she should do and found herself praying to God for the first time. Anything in the hope that this young mother and her small children would find health and happiness within this lifetime. She tried not to cry but tears inevitably pooled in her eyes.

There was a tap on her shoulder. She spun around to find John. He too had taken off his leather coat, gloves, and scarf. Matron stood behind him and was no longer wearing her scarf, and the nurse no longer had her bonnet on. They were piled in John's arms. She nodded to him and took the bundle. She helped the mother put on her husband's coat and clothes and swapped the old bonnet with the nurse's new one. When they had finished dressing the woman in their assortment of clothes, Miriam bowed her head. At the very least they could have some warming comfort this evening and perhaps could sell some of the items to help pay for more food.

But it didn't seem like enough. It wasn't enough. Why wasn't it enough?

"Come back tomorrow," Miriam whispered, hoping that the parent understood enough to listen. "I shall have more tomorrow."

The mother gave her a weak yet grateful smile. As the trio disappeared out of the hospital, Miriam felt her heart break. She tried to keep calm, but her hands were shaking. She watched the empty space where the poor family had been and soon a rush of tears cascaded down her face. She sniffed, desperate not to show weakness in front of everyone. Her husband's hand landed on her shoulder and gave her a kindly squeeze. His calming smell of lavender, mint, and chamomile yearned to comfort her also but instead, she was plunged into chaos.

With all her emotions overwhelming her, Miriam did not turn around. Instead, she sniffed again, and said, "Excuse me," before she ran out of the courtyard and into the hospital.

Chapter Three:

The Cupboard

John waited until everything was packed away before he went to find his wife.

He knew from experience that she needed the space to process her sorrow. She found it terribly difficult to cry in front of anyone at the hospital, especially in front of Matron and the nurses. She feared it would undercut her authority. Instead, she scurried herself away to a secret spot. Not that she had anything to fear, no one said a bad word about her leaving, even if it had meant that they had to tidy without her. In fact, as she had finished her shift, Nurse Barnard had taken time to speak on how much she admired Miriam for showing how much she cared unequivocally. "I hope to be a doctor just like her."

It made John's heart burst with pride.

He and Matron helped carry the empty vats and dirty dishes over to his office. Without Miriam, he gave Matron the gift that the pair had brought her – a new expensive gold broach that was shaped like her favourite bird – a robin. There were rubies sitting within its breast. To John's surprise, she thanked him with a gentle hug before she too left to experience the remains of Christmas with her sister's family.

Alone, John let out a sigh before he walked out of his office and through the Men's Building. He descended down a few flights of stairs to the first floor. The hospital was surprisingly quiet, with only a few admitted terminal or bed-ridden patients and their family members who had visited. The slimmed-down staff had mostly volunteered their time to keep an eye on those who remained and give treatment when necessary. The Bennetts, Sir Fredric, Matron and Michael remained on call – ready to be beckoned if there was an emergency.

John enormously enjoyed the near silence as his heeled shoe clacked against the floor. As he stepped down the long corridor, he found himself facing a familiar sight. A tiny cupboard that no one truly used. It was dingey. Two people could barely stand in it. It housed an assortment of hospital equipment: Shelves of jars and gauze and bandages. Yet it was rarely used, forgotten about within the regular hospital hubbub - relegated to being spare.

It had taken a whole two months of working there, and a month into his courtship with Miriam, before John was introduced to it. For this marvellous cupboard was, in fact, an exceptional place to contain their unruly and unescapable passions. Even if they were cramped in and had to get inventive with their positions.

But the cupboard had, in fact, another use. One greater than their copulations. A task which it upheld long before John had arrived at the Clayton Hospital. Being practically abandoned save for himself and his wife, Miriam utilised it as a hiding spot. For it was an excellent place to cry. He knew immediately that that was where she was hiding.

He hesitated a little bit, not entirely sure if she was ready to be seen. He wiggled his fingers before he knocked on the door. He didn't wait for a response before he gently pushed the cupboard door open.

"You found me," she said immediately as the light from the door fell upon her. She tried to be playful though there was a croak in her voice from crying. She was sitting on a stool, her face was red and blotchy, and there were tears still cascading down her face. She sniffed snot and wiped what she could with the back of her hand. He offered her a considerate smile, hoping that it would give her some comfort. "You all must've thought me a fool."

"My darling girl," he whispered gently as he closed the door behind him and crouched down in front of her. Reaching for her hands, he grabbed them fiercely. "We thought no such thing.. More concerned than anything…" John gave her a kindly squeeze before he reached up to her face and brushed away whatever fresh tears had toppled down her face. "What troubles you Miriam?"

He knew the answer before she even said it.

In the quietest voice, she hushed, "I cannot save them all."

She regretted the words slightly as her husband softly crinkled his eyes and gave her a light smile. His hand started to tuck her hair behind her ear in a relaxing fashion. She could not explain it entirely, but she did not wish to be comforted. She wanted to be perpetually angry. She wanted to feel this pain. She wanted to scream and shout at this unjust world. It did not help that John's response, however correct, only added to her frustrations. He said, "No Miriam, you cannot save them all."

Instead of allowing herself some peace and acceptance, she flew into a flurry of hot words, letting go of his hands so that she could gesticulate wildly. "What good is my stupid wealth and status if I cannot do that? All my life I have only known comfort and spoils whilst there are those out there like that poor mother and her children who'll only know suffering. For what reason John? Because they were born in different circumstances than I!? It is unfair and it is cruel."

She was so incensed that she roused the empty medical bottles. They clunked and rattled alongside her rage, as though they too were jeering in agreement. John allowed the tirade to swirl around the room before he reached up to her hands and again, clasped them as a way to calm her down. He knelt when crouching had gotten too sore. "May I tell you a story, Miriam?"

Snuffling, she nodded gently. "Of course, my dear John, anything."

"When I was nine, on Christmas Day, my mother could not raise enough money to buy us dinner. She tried very hard, mind, and worked long hours, but ultimately, she could not stretch her money. At the time we shared lodgings with a Polish family, who did not speak much English. Perhaps that is why my mother was too afraid to ask them for help or perhaps she was too proud. Regardless, we ventured out on a cold, bitter Christmas day." He paused so he could take a deep breath and calm the memory that were brewing within. "We managed to find soup at a kitchen quite like the one you made today. It was measly, but it was warm enough to stave off the chill. However, when we arrived back at our lodgings, to our surprise, the family had made an entire feast in the front room and warmly greeted us. Well… as big of a feast as they could manage… but so much more than what we were expecting. They invited us to dine with them and join in their festivities. They had even knitted me, and my mother, scarves as presents. They asked for nothing in return. Just that we eat and be merry."

Miriam let out a soft gasp. "You have never told me that before."

"I have never told anyone." John swallowed to coat over the fresh quaking emotions that had emerged. He had told Miriam a lot about his childhood – the candle, the poverty, and eventually, the abuse – but it seemed he had not uncovered all of his wounds to her. "The point I am striving to make is that I will always remember and be grateful for the kindness we were shown that day. As I am most certain that mother and her children will remember your generosity. To you, it may not seem like much, but to them, it will be everything."

Miriam did not respond. Instead, she allowed his story to swim through her. Quite thoughtlessly, she sometimes forgot that her husband did not come from wealth like she did. Instead, for the first years of his life, he had lived in poverty. Then he had spent years in the clutches of his abhorrent aunt. He had pulled himself through the worst of times to become the well-respected and kind surgeon that she knew today. And here he was, giving her comfort, as she wailed about the state of the world. She sniffed again and tried to dispel her tears. She feared the situation did not need any more. "Forgive me."

"There is nothing to forgive." He moved to one knee so that he could lean up and kiss her on her very wet cheek. "We can go home if you so wish."

Miriam shook her head. "That would terribly upset Father and Aunt Isobel. They have probably been hard at work putting an entire dinner together."

"Very well." He reached into his waistcoat for his gold pocket watch. "I believe their carriage is due to collect us in fifteen minutes." As he slid the watch back, he smirked and wiggled his eyebrows. "That should allow us some time if you so desire to utilise this cupboard for other activities."

"John!" Miriam exclaimed and playfully slapped him on the shoulder. She knew he did not mean it, not really anyway. She was too mopey and pouting to engage in sex right now. What he had done, however, was make her laugh.

And if there was one thing the world needed, it was more laughter.

Chapter Four:

The Snow

The carriage picked them up promptly at three.

 The chill in the air had turned into snow. Small flecks of white spiralling down from the grey above. Outside of the hospital, standing awkwardly by the huge vats, John held onto his hat and marvelled upwards at the sight. A particularly huge snowflake raced down and hit his nose, causing him to shake and erupt into a broad smile.

 Clutching onto two presents in a wicker basket, Miriam giggled as she watched him. She held out one of her gloveless hands to catch specks in her palm. As the biting coldness met her skin, she could only think of that poor mother and her children. The weather was harsher now for them if they did not have proper shelter. Miriam swallowed nervously, desperate not to cry again but she was also overcome with emotions.

She could have done more. She should have done more. Why didn't she do more?

When the soft clop of horse hooves echoed closer to them, Miriam tried to place the thoughts to the back of her mind. She told herself that if the mother did not return to the hospital tomorrow, then she would at least head into the streets and try to find her. As the hansom cab pulled into view, a shaky breath escaped her lips and steamed immediately into the air.

However, as she saw the driver, she could not help but smile. She was so excited that she almost dropped the basket of presents that she was holding when she started waving profusely. When the cab stopped in front of them, she said brightly, "WINSTON! What the devil are you doing working on Christmas Day? I must have words with my aunt."

The man laughed as he hopped down from the back of the hansom cab. He was tall and stocky with no visible hair underneath his hat. He wore a huge brown coat and matching gloves. He tipped his hat to Miriam. "Merry Christmas, Doctor Bennett..." His Essex accent stretched across his words as he beamed brightly. He then tipped his hat to John. "... and Doctor Bennett." John responded in kind, adding a polite nod as well. Winston then turned back to Miriam. "You know as well as I do that I cannot say no to Lady Grey."

"All the same," Miriam exclaimed as she suddenly wrapped her arms around the man and brought him into a cordial embrace. "I hope she is paying you handsomely for your troubles."

"Oh but of course!" He smiled as they parted from the hug. He bent down and started lifting the vats and equipment onto the front of the cab with John's help. Winston Longmuir had been Aunt Isobel's chauffeur for the past year. From their conversations, Miriam had established that he had been a widow for five years now, with one grown-up son around Miriam's age, who lived in the middle of the country. He made a comfortable living from being a private chauffeur. He was already well-known within the family for his cheery disposition and unequivocal kindliness. As he guided Miriam into the cab, he said, "I have had a sneak at your dinner and your father has truly outdone himself."

Sitting down, she placed the presents on the chair opposite before she replied, "Oh wonderful, will you be joining us?"

"Alas, my son and his family are visiting later so no but I shall pop by to take you home this evening."

"You are a true treasure," Miriam said, reaching over and gripping his hand tightly.

When the cab started trotting down to Clapham, Miriam wrapped both of her arms around one of John's and leaned upon his shoulder. She let out a sigh that was moored between two different emotions – sadness and contentment. It escaped into the carriage and denoted that she needed the silence to contemplate and regain her spirit. He wordlessly agreed, having a fondness for the quiet anyway, and instead turned to gaze out the window.

The world trotted by like a scenic greeting card.

London truly looked beautiful in the sheen of twinkling white, as though the snow could mask its faults and follies. He had lived there for nearly two decades but was often at odds with the usual busyness and the chaos, even though he centred himself in the middle of the fray. He appreciated the city but in a different way than most. He admired the place for how it accepted a lot of his wickedness and gifted him a wondrous night life that matched his own decadence. He idolized the secret places which housed his fervent desires. Most of all, he greatly loved how the city had given him her, especially as she too was a child of darkness.

In the snow, he could see how sparkling the daylight was. The centre itself was bereft of most people, so the snow settled on the usually muddy and wet streets without disturbance.

As they left the city centre and trotted down more residential streets, he could see how jolly the weather was. People left their homes to play. It was almost as though each flake of snow possessed an indescribable magic. Every time one landed upon a person; the tragedy of adulthood melted. Within this childlike fascination, even the coldest of hearts would allow themselves to smile. He watched the openness and exuberance as people held onto each other closely. He saw the children ball up the snow and throw them gleefully at one another. He could smell the cooked treats of nearby vendors and could still hear the sound of choirs singing. Christmas was, indeed, more mystical than he could have ever dreamed.

Miriam snuggled against her husband's arm. She did not watch the noise of the outside. Instead, she quietly turned upwards to John. There were many moments with her husband where she found herself loving him more. He had a manner about him that treated life as though it were still an extraordinary thing. Nearing forty, she would've expected him to be done with such trivial things such as hope and joy like most men were. Especially a man who had been shown such cruelty and abandonment. Yet here he was, staring out of their carriage, shuffling excitedly at the snow as it fell down on the streets.

As they were pulled away from the city centre, Miriam wound herself further against him and watched his excited eyes dart back and forth outside. The small sense of a smile that he kept buried underneath his moustache. With the rocking of the carriage and that enchanting lavender aroma, Miriam found her eyelids were heavy. Her turbulent mind and her calamitous heart were soothed into an unexpected nap.

"Darling, we are here."

Miriam stirred. She tried to open her eyes and found them closing again. After crying so much during the day, her eyelids were heavy, and it seemed an impossible task. The carriage had indeed stopped and there was silence as John waited for her to rise. Instead, she moaned a little and curled into her husband's arm, wishing to fall asleep again. "Perhaps I should leave you here and have dinner all by myself."

"Perhaps you should be quiet," Miriam huffed but offered him a smile. With great force, she pushed her eyes open and unfurled herself from John. She blinked as the daylight seemed brighter against the white. Looking out the carriage window by her seat, she could see that Clapham Common had been completely covered in snow. There were still flakes trickling down from the sky. She then looked across at her husband. Winston was already removing the vats and carefully plodding through the snow down the pathway of her father's townhouse and in through the open front door. Miriam sighed. She feared she was not quite ready to be jolly and merry.

"We can still leave," John whispered suddenly as though he read her mind entirely, "There is no shame in saying you are unwell."

She contemplated the possibility. There was a call that beckoned her home. She thought how peaceful it would be to just lie in bed with her husband for the rest of the day, instead of forcing herself to be. Her father and aunt would surely understand.

All of the plans for the day, all of those fantasies, and all of the surprises she had in store for later that evening, they struck her immediately. Her stomach even barked as she thought about all the luscious food her father had prepared. Shaking her head, Miriam let out a final sigh. "No, I believe the best remedy is to be around family right now."

"Quite right." John leaned over and kissed her on the cheek. There was an air of pure excitement in his words that made it even more crucial that she rallied for the day. He was practically bouncing as he scooped up the basket and carefully stepped out of the carriage. His shoes crunched as they hit the snow. He held out his hand to guide her slowly onto the already slippery pavement.

As she slid her arm through his, they made their way up the pathway. The four-storey high townhouse had a small front garden that had a few trees and bushes that the Claytons had allowed to grow almost unkempt and wild so their home could be shrouded somewhat from the city. A reflection of their manor house in the countryside. Thanks to the snow, the front garden was covered in white and looked like a perfect painting of winter. It was, however, curious that the front door was open yet there was no one waiting to receive them. Quite often, Sir Fredric would be waiting to greet them heartily. There was no one in the frame of the door. Perhaps he was too busy with cooking and had forgotten about their arrival. She cocked her head curiously.

That is when she heard a tiny chortle from behind one of the bushes which caused the branches to shake. She should have known better. There was little time to react when she saw her father's arm emerge from the leaves. A whoosh of air preceded his attack. She let go of her husband and ducked. John was not so lucky. A ball of cold snow hit him square in the face which, in turn, knocked his hat off his head.

He stood dumbfounded by what had happened. With one hand he clutched onto the basket handle and with the other, he wiped the wet sludge from his face.

Miriam could not help but laugh at him as she picked up his hat and placed it back on his head. She sat her words underneath a whisper so that her father could not hear. "See, it is not pleasant when something hits you unexpectedly."

A flickering memory paced between them, causing both John and Miriam to grin goofily.

Another whoosh. This time Miriam was the target, and she wasn't fast enough. It smashed on her chest. She exclaimed before she bent down to the ground and scooped up her own ball. "Right, this is war Father!"

She launched the snow fiercely at the bush which caused Sir Fredric to scurry out of hiding. The stocky man may have looked his age – with grey mutton chops, a bushy huge moustache, and a bed of white hair on his head – but he most certainly did not act it. When her retaliating shot missed and splodged against the window, she tutted out of irritation. Another shot from Sir Fredric, but the older man had overshot, and the ball glided over the heads of the Bennetts.

Miriam huffed and bent down to roll another bit of snow. With her father now in plain sight, she was certain that she could hit him at least once. She went to throw but was surprised to see another had landed squarely on Sir Fredric's nose before she could. He guffawed loudly. Miriam turned to find that John had placed the basket of presents down and was already re-arming, bending down for more icy ammo. She had never seen quite a gigantic grin on his face which caused her heart to skip a beat.

Unfortunately, what she did not anticipate was being her husband's new target. When he stood back up, he pelted the snowball right at her. It landed on her face, breaking the bitter cold slush across her cheeks. John snorted before he burst into loud chuckles.

"Now it is war upon you both!" she shrieked.

There was no relent. The three of them were engaged in a winter warfare, running and ducking around the front garden, shooting snowballs in all directions. John's hat had fallen off once more and remained lodged in the icy ground. Miriam's dress was soaking from the amount of times it was hit. Sir Fredric's nose was bright red. Their laughter was lighter than anything and echoed around the whole of Clapham.

It was about ten minutes of battle before a shrill voice sounded out from the doorway, "Erm excuse me, children!"

Lady Grey, or Aunt Isobel as she preferred to be known in less formal settings, stood with folded arms in the shadow of the front door. Winston stood beside her, with a gentle hand on her shoulder, as they gawked at the scene in front of them. Though her tone had been stern, Isobel was smiling. Miriam nodded. "I am sorry Izzy, but Father started it!"

"I am most certain that he did," The old slight woman patted her neatly poised grey hair then beckoned them in with a big hand gesture. "Come now, let us get you warm. I have just made hot chocolate."

"Oh!" Miriam said, not dropping her childlike façade for a second. She scooped up the basket of presents and bounded in through the door ahead of everyone, even pushing by Isobel and

Winston as they said their goodbyes. Her husband and father trudged in after her.

Immediately, her father's home embraced her, wrapping around her spirit with the utmost comfort. A sigh of relief fell from her lips. The pains and the years melted away. She felt youthful and energised again, ready to open more presents that this Christmas could offer.

Chapter Five:

The Feast

Since Miriam was a child, her father had always cooked Christmas Dinner.

For most of the year, he allowed others to do the job. At their Manor in Northamptonshire, their much beloved housekeeper Hettie did most of the meals. In their Clapham Townhouse, it was their not-as-good housekeeper Mrs Smith. However, Sir Fredric was a man who often went against his station. He dismissed his staff, with full pay, on Christmas Day so that they could have the time with their respective families.

It meant that every Christmas, he could finally do what he really secretly liked: Cooking a full hearty meal for his dear family. He was very good at it too, though not quite up to Hettie's standards.

Today was no exception. Despite the fact that he had also cooked for the charity drive, he still had time to make an almost lavish feast. The biggest Christmas Dinner that John had ever had in his life. When he sat down, he ogled all the piles of dishes like a child hankering for confectionary. Never in his life had he seen such a display of glorious food. There were three different types of potatoes from mashed to boiled to roasted. Different bowls of vegetables dotted around the table in hues of green, yellow, and orange. In the centre sat a ham joint and a goose, cooked so perfectly that steam still simmered from the brazed golden meat. Plus there were dishes filled with gravy to pour on their food and plenty of red wine. The minute he smelled them, John's stomach whinged.

They sat around Sir Fredric's slight dining room table. As it was merely a party of four, there was no protest to Miriam and John being nestled against one another. Isobel and Sir Fredric sat on the other side.

Dinner began with a sweet silence to Miriam's late mother Anna, who died shortly after Miriam was born. It was followed by a grace before Sir Fredric encouraged them all to dig in and plentifully as well. The food was so delicious and so great that no one uttered a word for two rounds. They just feasted on the succulent meat and drank heartily at very rich red wine. With every bite, John wordlessly said his own prayers. He was gripped with a great gratitude that he could be here around this table, revelling in the prosperity this family had to offer. He happily accepted seconds and would even contemplate a third plate.

Miriam, however, stuck with just the one. When he asked her why she was tempering her usual abundant appetite, she shrugged nonchalantly. "Rather busy night ahead. I do not wish to feel bloated and ghastly."

The sentence made John stop at a second helping.

He did not think they had anything other than this dinner.

It meant that either she was thinking of the woman at the hospital still and felt guilty for letting her go or she had a sensational plan for their evening that she was keeping guarded. Knowing Miriam as well as he did, the answer was probably both.

"Would you like to take some home with you?" Sir Fredric enquired as Miriam scooped up the leftover food to take into the kitchen. When she didn't answer immediately, he nodded his head. "Or perhaps you would prefer to come round tomorrow to take to the hospital for patients and anyone in need?"

Miriam kissed Sir Fredric on the cheek. "You read my mind Father."

Aunt Isobel had only started attending their Christmas Dinners ten years ago, three years after her husband Charles had died. Lord Charles Grey was a particularly violent and controlling man. In the years following his death, Isobel had tried to unravel from his ghost. After much encouragement, she had travelled to London to join them for Christmas dinner but was timid and withdrawn. Also, a tad appalled at the lack of servants, despite Sir Fredric's title and wealth.

Now she always made the dessert.

Every year she would outdo herself with a stunning creation, as well as the traditional plum pudding. This year she opted for riband jelly. An almost sweet masterpiece creation that looked like a pink and yellow fortress that quaked as she brought it towards the table.

Miriam made sure there was plenty of furore for Aunt Isobel when she brought out the dish and served it to everyone. The light dessert looked delectable.

Upon his first bite, John moaned quietly beside her. Not loud enough for the room to hear, but enough for Miriam to notice. It was a soft note of appreciation. A familiar sound which fell upon her skin and sunk deep into the senses. She took a bite and found that her hand was slightly shaking. As the sweet jelly coated her tongue, she hoped to distract herself with the dessert but soon enough, she heard John sighed in an almost heavenly way.

She cocked her head to watch her husband and instantly regretted doing so. John was a man of great appreciation. He drank good wine as though it were his last drink, he smoked cigars as though he were to die tomorrow, and he ate food as if he had been starved all his life. Taking bites of this dessert was no different: He moved his mouth across his spoon, appreciating each morsel. At points, he even closed his eyes so that he could savour solely the taste of the jelly. As she watched, all she could think about was how his tongue could do awful, terrible, and brilliant things to her body.

A heat spread between her legs, and she wriggled uncomfortably on the chair. She tried to concentrate on eating her own food, if anything to cool her hot ideas. She even picked up the dessert wine and chugged almost the entire contents to drown the cacophony of need inside of her. All the while she tried to hide the fact that she was having decadent thoughts about her husband.

"Oh my goodness," Isobel exclaimed, her spoon clattering to the bowl which made them all jump slightly and stare at her. She took her napkin from her lap and folded it on the table. "I forgot all about the plum pudding! Freddie, could you please help me bring it in?"

Sir Fredric, who nearly on his fourth bite, pouted a little bit as he placed it back down resigned. He nodded and soon enough the pair were walking to the kitchen.

Miriam followed their departure before she flipped her attention back around to John, her eyes wide and pleading. "You best stop."

John cocked his head as he sneakily scooped another bite. "Stop what?"

A flustered red unfurled on her cheek as she flapped an accusatory finger at him. "That."

"What the devil are you…" Then it dawned on John. He snickered. "Oh… I see." He dug his spoon deep into the jelly for another bite. Her deep blue eyes followed his actions. He strengthened his stare as he slowly raised the cutlery into his mouth and dragged his plush lips gradually across the silver as he pulled it out. He then licked the cream from his lips. Smiling slyly, he flashed a wink in her direction and watched as her mouth dropped open. "Too titillating for you Miriam?"

"Oh, you ratbag!" She playfully kicked him in the shins which did nothing to alleviate the mischievous grin that had formed. She yearned to tease him back, rile him in the same manner in which he had roused her. Get him hot under the collar and sweating for a taste of her body. So she hung her next sentence low. "Perhaps we *should* take some home to see how sweet it would taste if eaten from my nude form."

"A delightful idea, Miriam," John said, and a sprig of pink blossomed on his cheeks. He pushed his thigh so that it settled against hers, allowing their excitements to pass between them. He cast his sights to the door and tried to assess his next action. Satisfied that there was still time, he waved two fingers in front of her before he plunged them into his dessert, scooping up a chunk of pink jelly, and placing it into his mouth with a small whine. John's eyes never stopped staring, watching intently as she nibbled on her bottom lip.

Oh, he was good.

He was very, very good.

And she was impossibly wet.

Miriam dithered slightly as her entire body tensed. She went to the counter with something to regain her dominance, but the doors of the dining room burst open and there was a very loud cheer. The Bennetts separated as though they were caught in a salacious arrangement, both turning as burgundy as the wine.

They snapped their attention to the head of the table. Quite proudly stood Sir Fredric and Aunt Isobel. Together, they were presented the plum pudding which, thanks to a hearty helping of rum, was completely ablaze. Both older family members were grinning broadly at the surprise as it burned vividly and brightly in front of them all.

Remembering herself, Miriam took a deep breath to dispel her filthy fantasies. She clapped very hurriedly and heartily. "Oh bravo, Izzy. Stupendous."

"Y-y-yes," John stammered, and he raised a toast to the display. "Magnificent."

Isobel beamed brightly. She carefully placed the plum pudding in the centre. Sir Fredric sat back down and immediately dug into the jelly that he had been unwillingly parted from. When the flames subsided, Isobel sliced into the brown stodgy cake and gave them all a hearty helping. With the generous helping of jelly still wobbling in her bowl, Miriam let out a small gasp. She was torn. Her sweet tooth yearned to the song of the dessert as though it were a starved sailor being beckoned by a siren. Yet she did not want to feel too full for the evening. Not when she wished to fuck her husband all night long after her dastardly master plan was finally revealed. So she took steady and pragmatic bites, moving the food around her dish to make it look as if she was eating plentifully.

John wasn't making it easier on her either. Now armed with the knowledge that he could lure her to longing simply by eating slowly, he relished every single bite that he took. What's more, he had wriggled a foot free from his shoe and was skimming her ankles with his toes, rubbing across her stockings and up her calves which produced light butterfly-like sensations to flutter across her skin.

Every now and then, John tried to and gain the upper hand in all of their flirting and games. Like a petulant child would when being told what to do. A choice word, a wrong turn, or a rule break. He wanted to see her falter and he wanted to see how creative her punishments were when he was successful. At this moment, she was tempted to take her fork and plunge it into his thighs so he could feel a little pain.

Instead, she purposefully dropped the cutlery to the floor.

"Oh my goodness, do forgive me!" she exclaimed and before anyone could answer her, she dove to retrieve the fork. As she did, she gripped John's knee and dragged her left hand down his right leg. When she had reached the fork, leaning her head on his lap underneath the table, she took the instrument and placed the prongs on his leg. Then as she slowly rose from under the table, she dragged the tip of the fork upwards.

It took a lot of willpower from John not to come in his trousers. He dared not react. He could barely say anything. He simply stared blankly across the table. Both Isobel and Sir Fredric had initially looked bemused at Miriam's accident before they chatted once more about their recipes. John tried to focus on the food again, but he was practically being tortured. The four-pointed tips ran along the outside of his trousers and yet produced unforgettable feelings like sparks of electricity across his body. As she rolled the fork over his knee, he twitched and let out a small gasp. He found himself yearning to be speared in the flesh with the cutlery.

"There we are!"

When she sat back up, she huffed upon the silver and rubbed her fork with her napkin. As she started to eat again, she sneakily placed her hand on his thigh and gave it a tender squeeze.

Oh, she was good.

She was very, very good.

And he was impossibly stiff.

They were both thankful when the dessert course had finished. As Sir Fredric and Lady Grey had provided the food, Miriam and John were to wash the dishes. A fair exchange that had become a bit of a tradition. The older pair ventured to the front room for a small tipple of sherry and to unwind from all of their hard work. Miriam had almost immediately started piling up bowls to take to the kitchen, humming under her breath.

John, however, stayed still underneath the table.

She clocked this immediately and laughed. "Come on John, you are not exempt from cleaning."

"I…" He coughed and looked around nervously. "I need a moment."

Miriam blinked before she threw her head back and cackled wildly. When her giggling had subsided, she arched her head to the living room door to make sure it was firmly shut. With no signs of her father and aunt coming back, she huffed out an uneasy sigh before she faced him and stepped over his legs. After a few seconds, she lifted her skirts and lowered her entire crotch upon his. He was right - he was practically tearing through his trousers. It made her privates twinge in excitement. She was very close to pulling him out of his confines and taking him there at the table. Instead, she rocked upon him. "Oh my, Doctor Bennett."

He let out a long-suffering moan, placing his hands on her hips, partly to stop her and partly because to stop himself from entering her. He could feel her wetness through the gap in her drawers as it soaked the material of his trousers, giving him another reason to stay fixed beneath the table. He turned his awe-filled gaze upwards to his brilliant wife and could see all the smutty images that rolled behind those alluring deep blue eyes of hers. "You best stop…"

"Agreed," she said as she bounced off him as though they were not hankering for the other so very much. Looking down, she could see the damp patch that she had left behind. She hummed a little as she began scooping up the remaining dishes and felt the heated almost glare of her husband on the side of her face. With a lopsided grin, she picked up a clothed napkin and threw it on his crotch. "There is a laundry basket upstairs, why not take the napkins and tablecloths up there before you join me in the kitchen?"

Before he could respond, Miriam had flounced out of the dining room and started cluttering with the plates, leaving him uncompleted. He balled up the fabric from the table and held it low to cover his burden.

As the chair scraped across the floor, he sighed. Perhaps this was her way of giving him permission to touch himself upstairs. He desperately needed relief if he were to try and be civilised for the rest of the evening. After all, he was impure of heart and completely ravenous. However, his carnal thoughts must've been loud and chaotic as the door opened. Miriam's head popped out and she grinned. "No. I shall have absolutely none of that, thank you very much."

When she disappeared again, John was more frustrated than ever.

Chapter Six:

The Candle

It had taken him a whole ten minutes before he was able to rejoin the family.

He sat on the edge of the bed and gripped the mattress tightly. Closing his eyes, he tried to rid himself from his stiffness by thinking about surgery. At first, he found it successful. After all, it was hardly scintillating to picture scalpels and disinfectants and aprons and blood and bodies. Yet she crept into his mind very easily. Those secret times in his surgery, the way his hands ran across her body, and the near-surgical way he could make her climax. One man could not have this much lust for his own wife, surely? He thought he was about to explode. At the very least, sequester himself in this room for the entire holiday. He even deliberated running out and falling against the snow to cool his arousal.

In the end, his solution was sport.

To soften his erection, he found himself reciting this year's cricket test scores.

When he had finally emerged from the room, Miriam had done half of the dishes. He picked up a tea towel and started to dry them. He was quite hesitant being close beside her because she was an impossible tease. Sure enough, she did not talk to him directly. Instead, she sang a little festive ditty as she cleaned the dishes and made sure to tease him. She brushed up against him when she skirted by, leaned over him so that her breasts pressed into his body, and when he bent down to put something in a low cupboard, she even squeezed his buttocks. He kept himself cool, calm, and collected though by the time they had finished cleaning, he was practically yelling the cricket scores to quell his need.

The pair joined the rest of the family in the living room for an evening glass of sherry. Night had settled in, so the room was drenched in an alluring amber. Against the backdrop of forest green and Sir Fredric's cluttered walls, there was an indescribable warm-heartedness. As Jon was invited to join Miriam on the settee, he felt a tugging in his heart. A wave of acceptance and belonging that he dare not spook away. No Christmas night had ever felt so comforting as though he had always belonged in such a small yet special family. In some ways, he hated how long it took him to get here. But he was here now, and he was determined to make the most of it.

It was finally time to exchange presents. The family opted for only one each and they drew names for whomever was going to buy for them. This Christmas night, Sir Fredric was to buy for

John, John was to buy for Aunt Isobel, Aunt Isobel had Miriam, and Miriam had her father. It was tradition to start with the youngest, but Miriam insisted on saving John's for last as she passed her present to Sir Fredric. She had gotten her old man a new and almost regal shaving kit for his facial hair. The handles were jade to match his favourite colour, and he was very happy with them. He gave Miriam a tight embrace.

John handed Aunt Isobel her gift next. He had purchased for her new and expensive oil paints. Miriam had told him that Isobel took to painting landscapes whenever she felt troubled. It brought her great peace. She, too, was extremely grateful for the thoughtful gift as she reached over and squeezed John's hand.

To everyone's surprise, Aunt Isobel had brought Miriam a new cape. This time it was a crisp autumnal orange velvet cape with a white fur trim. The ties were moulded to look like the fruit. There was gold threaded throughout the fabric. She raised the garment to show everyone, and found underneath the cape, there were matching gloves underneath. Miriam gasped when she saw them all, tracing her fingertips across the material as her mouth gaped open. Dumbfounded, she turned around to Isobel. "How did you know I would give mine away?"

Aunt Isobel smiled and softened her eyes. "A hunch. You almost always do," Isobel chuckled, "Do try to keep hold of these ones for a while though."

Miriam flung herself off from the settee to wrap her arms around Isobel fiercely. She cuddled the older woman tightly. Watching this scene unfold sent a strange comforting calm over John. He knew that whatever Miriam opened, she would've treated it as though it were a prized jewel. Yet he was oddly pleased that she was given something so fitting. So much so that he nearly thanked Isobel as well. Instead, he watched with a slight awe.

Miriam was fifteen when she and her father had moved to permanently live in London, so she did not have many childhood memories in this townhouse. Still, sitting around a Christmas tree, he couldn't help but picture what she was like as a curious child or tyrannical teenager. Would she boisterously march her father into the streets to help the needy? Did she excitedly peel open presents and exclaim loudly at the gifts? When was her first sip of wine and what was her favourite dessert when she was young? He couldn't wait to discover all the stories of her past. They had already shared so much in their short time together but there was more to explore. He wanted to colour in the between the lines and know each detail as though it were his own memory. Every second she was gloriously in this world. He watched to capture it all. A beautiful picture of his wife.

When she sat back down, she caught him staring, differently to how he was at dinner. She could not quite describe it, but it was as though he were in deep veneration. Thankful to simply be in this home, let alone receiving food and presents. She thought about the younger version of her husband. One that had suffered so much so young. The difference of harsh winters: Ones where he had to stave off the cold and the others where he had to stave off abuse. It surprised Miriam to think of him this way for this was where he belonged. He sat in her father's home and Miriam felt as though he had always been there – with her always. Like one of the many photographs on her father's wall – caught in time forever. She found herself blushing as she held the cape against her lap and slightly nudging him with her shoulder.

She nodded over to her father who handed his present to John. Sir Fredric had a lot of talents, but gift-giving was not one of them. In fact, when Miriam had started to deviate from toys, she found she had to direct him in presents. That was all the same with John's gift today. To her father's credit, he had tried for a couple of weeks before he surrendered and asked her for assistance. Sir Fredric handed John a long, slender green box that had a red bow stuck to one of the corners.

There was no paper to peel back. Instead, John lifted the lid to reveal the present. He immediately froze which caused Miriam's heart to stop. Inside the box was a long red candle which she had asked to have years painted on in gold. At the very top was 1895 and the numbers ascended until the very bottom, which was 1925. Thirty years was all the painter could squeeze on, but she was determined to replace this one when 1925 came around and they were old and greying. Nestled beside the candle was a small bar of chocolate.

John had not stirred for a while from staring at the gift.

The rest of the family eyed each other curiously.

Miriam's stomach twisted and she feared that she had gotten it completely wrong.

It was her father who broke the silence as he boomed, "Something the matter, Bennett?"

"N-n-no..." John said as his voice broke. When he turned to Sir Fredric, Miriam could see there were fresh tears in his eyes. They shimmered in the fire's glow. "I am... This is... How did you know?"

Sir Fredric smiled and gently gestured his head to Miriam who felt as though a stage spotlight suddenly shone on her face. As John turned to face her, she could see that his eyes were watery with tears on the edge of his eyelashes, and his chin scrunched. She found herself flying into excuses. "I thought we could share your tradition. A new beginning for this new family."

She reached over and grabbed one of his hands. He squeezed it tightly as she delicately glided her thumb over his fingers. John placed the candle between them so he could compose himself. He reached over for his sherry, bending over the arm of the chair to the table beside him in hopes he could skim away his tears without anyone noticing. Miriam did and found she had a greater fondness for the man. When he sat back down properly, he straightened his suit and smiled at his wife with utmost devotion.

"This means a great deal to me," John finally replied shakily to Sir Fredric as he stood up and walked over to his father-in-law to shake his hand. "Thank you so much."

As he sat back down, Aunt Isobel chimed, "Shall we light it now? I think that would be rather splendid with all of us here."

They all agreed. John pulled the candle from the box. Sir Fredric rummaged in one of his drawers to find a tiny silver yet ornate holder. He placed it on the mantle. John leaned the white roped wick into a flame of another candle and held it there until it was finally alight. Then placing it on the holder, he passed them all a small bit of chocolate before he stepped back so they could gather around.

There this little family stood together watching as the candle fluxed through the first year. They all made the same promise, that as long as life allowed it, they would find themselves together. Perhaps in a different home. Perhaps with others who would join their funny little unit. Perhaps with children that one day Miriam and John would have. But they will always find their way here, watching his candle slowly dissolve through the years.

What a jubilant occasion.

For they were together, and they were grateful to be alive.

And together, they elevated their glasses to toast the moment.

Miriam leaned against his shoulder.

In turn, John rested his head against his wife's.

They sighed contentedly in harmony.

Whilst they watched the flame devour the current year, both of the Bennetts glanced excitedly and mused on the years to come. The years that they would surely spend like this.

Together.

Chapter Seven:

The Presents

It had just rolled by eight o'clock when the Bennetts returned to their home.

When they arrived in their townhouse near St James' Park, it was solidly night. The onyx sky was cleared of clouds, so the snow had stopped falling. The darkness skirted over the white causing it to sparkle like the bright stars.

Miriam sighed blissfully when they walked into the warmth as she undid her cape and placed it upon the clothes hook. As she removed her bonnet, causing her hair to protrude wildly, John discarded his top hat and rushed forward furiously. The door thumped behind him. Despite the fact that he was filled with food and love from the dinner, he found he was utterly and unforgivably ravenous for her. Wrapping his arms around her waist, he pulled her against him so she could feel how wanting he was through his layers.

She did not wriggle free or squeal like she sometimes did. Instead, she circled her hips against him and purred, "You are very desperate for me it seems."

"I always am." He nestled his words against her neck, following the letters with his lips. He needed her now – even if that meant pushing her against the staircase and taking her there. He ran one of his hands down her body, ready to roll up her skirts and feel how damp her drawers were, certain he could feel her wetness already. He let out a moan as he kissed what little skin she had on display.

Suddenly, a loud bang echoed from upstairs.

John froze. "What was that?"

As if there was nothing but silence in the air, Miriam sprang free from his clasp and headed to the stairs. Sitting down to take her boots off, she nonchalantly replied, "What was what?"

"That sound just now." Bewildered, he stood in the middle of the hallway before he took a step forward and glanced upwards to see if he could find a source. "Did you not hear that bang?"

She struggled and strained with her boots. "Hmm, no but perhaps it was just the wind knocking something over in the spare room. These old houses are so creaky, do you not think?

John studied her features and tried to assess her countenance, not quite believing her. There was something so mischievous there in her smile. He frowned. "Miriam—"

"Oh John!" she exclaimed and clapped her hands together a little bit. She leaped up from the stairs and grabbed his hands, pulling him through to the living room. "We have not done our own presents yet, have we?"

The fireplace was already on. He could not remember if they had extinguished it in the morning. Yet there it was, blazing a golden hue that illuminated their front room. Their home had been decorated for the festive season. Nestled in the alcove of their big bay window was a gigantic tree that skimmed the surface of the ceiling. They had spent a glorious Sunday in early December placing fine new baubles, silky red and gold ribbons, and an assortment of figurines. There was no rhyme nor pattern to how they draped the decorations which they both admitted made the tree look and feel more Christmassy. Miriam treasured this. Finally, her scatty nature made something more beautiful.

They had even dressed green and red paper chains across the walls and above the fireplace.

There were not many presents under the tree. In fact, there was just one. A thin and long wrapped wooden box. John's gift to Miriam. As she dragged him over, he was a tad surprised. He had not expected much but she had been teasing him for a good week that she would be triumphant in their gifts to one another, as though it were some naughty game they were playing. So, seeing nothing bar his own present to her was a shock. It twisted in his stomach with a cocktail of excitement, and he tried to stifle a smile. She had a conniving plan – he could practically see it dance within her eyes alongside the flames.

If that was the case, he was more than excited to hand her over his gift. As if she were a happy youth, she sat down on the floor, her red skirt billowing out across the dark brown wood. John had poured them both a glass of neat smoky whisky and joined her too beneath the tree. His cheeks grew heated as she fumbled at the paper. He sipped at the golden liquor to distract himself as she unearthed a long shiny mahogany box. There was a golden latch keeping the lid locked tight. She curiously ran her hands across the wood as though the box itself was enough of a gift. Then she fiddled with the latch and sprung the lid open.

Lying inside, nestled against red velvet were three leather riding crops and whips. There was one with a stubby black handle that had several lengthy pieces of leather protruding from the top. There was a midsize one which had a curved look of the same black material. Finally, there was the longest one nestled in the middle, which had a tapered rectangle, almost like a gift tag. She carefully danced her fingertips across each instrument with the utmost satisfaction. "John, they are exquisite."

"Apologies," he said into the glass, steaming up the sides with his heated breath and sordid ideas, "for I fear they are as much a present for myself as they are for you."

"Thank you ever so much." She gave him a lopsided grin which caused his heart to falter. It began to thud even more erratically when she dropped her smile. The gilded reflection of the fire caused shadows to skulk across her face, changing her demeanour and making her look as though she had fought through the flames to be there. "Shall we try one out?"

He swallowed the remnants of his drink, appreciating the searing down his gullet. He placed the glass to one side before he nodded. "Yes."

"Yes what?"

"Yes please goddess."

"Very good." Miriam watched him intently as her eyes darkened. She pushed herself up from the floor, discarding the box under the tree, and stood with the longest crop in her hand. He rose with her. She stroked the tip of the leather across her palms. She seemed at odds with her colourful quaint dress as her true form augmented through her body. "Assume the position John."

An electric shock bounded through him and corralled all of his cells into action. He could already feel a pinching beneath his trousers as his prick hardened slowly. Stepping over to his chair, he bent down over one arm and clutched onto the other tightly. There were no sounds save for the crackling of the fireplace, his now heavy breathing, and the fabric as it strained and creaked underneath his grasp.

She swished over to him in near silence. He could only tell she was nearby when her shadow fell across him. The intensity of her intentions loomed over him also. Especially when she slammed the implement into her palm. The smack of it caused him to jump, even though she had not hit him yet. Immediately, his dick grew against the arm. He held all the moans in his throat, even when she hit the crop into her hand again. Humming in approval, she whispered, "Roses to stop, remember?"

There was barely enough time for affirmation before she had brought the crop against his buttocks. It was a lenient touch – a trial to test the equipment. There was no more pain than if she had lightly tapped him on the arm. John's stomach twisted from the anticipation as she paused in the moment, tempting him with time.

Then she struck him again. A little bit harder this time. He grunted from the slight smarting that appeared upon his skin. Another brief pause because she hit him with a bigger force, producing a bigger smattering of pain. He gripped tightly onto the chair as a moan escaped his lips. She hit him again with the same strength, and again, and again. All with the same infliction, all producing the same intoxicating curl of agony.

There was another brief interlude.

She sucked in a breath. "Unbutton your trousers. I want to hear how it truly sounds across your arse."

John did as he was instructed. He lifted himself slightly from the chair and wasted little time taking off his colourful striped waistcoat. Then he unclasped his braces and skirted his trousers down, along with his underwear. He was careful not to show her his erection, not when she hadn't asked, and as he bent back down across the chair, it pressed against the fabric.

"Such an obedient servant you are for me."

The sentence made him bristle excitedly.

Finally he could hear a loud swoosh as she raised the crop into the air and brought it fast down against his buttocks. He cried out this time. Loudly. But he did not relent. Not when she struck him repeatedly. As hard as she could. The agony raced across him and shot through his penis. The friction of his erection against the sofa fabric caused a small bit of pre-ejaculate to emerge. Miriam continued, panting with the activity, as she slapped the crop against him. He cried with pain.

The pain.

Oh God.

The pain.

The sweet momentous pain.

The pain was finally too much.

"Roses!" he relented in a boisterous bellow.

She immediately stopped, taking deep breaths in the process. He slumped against the chair. She walked around and bent down in front of him, scooping up the loose hair that had escaped his tight waves and tucked it behind his ear. He breathed out a jagged breath.

She kissed his lips with sweet affection. "Are you alright?"

The level of care in her words enveloped his heartbeat as it carried on erratically. His member was entirely agonized. As he scrambled up from the armchair, it stood to attention, silhouetted by the orange flames. "More than alright," he croaked out.

He questioned when she would give him alleviation and exactly how. She rose slowly before she dragged her eyes from his face to his erection and back up again. There was no discernible tone as she said, "Do up your trousers for now."

The instruction was perplexing. As he tucked his needy penis away into his colourful trousers with a soft moan. Pulling his braces back over his shoulder, and fiddling with the clasps, he frowned. Almost always, his brutalised reprimands were met with some sort of remuneration.

Instead, Miriam placed the crop back in the box and wiped the sweat from her brow. She picked up his abandoned glass and poured him another drink. Walking over to him, she handed him the whisky and, as always, had read his mind. She answered with a smirk. "You shall get your reward soon enough. After all, I believe it is time for your present."

Miriam had disappeared from the living room for half an hour.

John sat in his armchair, shuffling to smooth his sore skin. He gripped tightly onto his glass as though it were the only thing keeping him in place. There had been a confusing number of sounds in her absence which had caused a mixture of excitement and trepidation to knot his stomach. At first, it was just her excited footsteps and creaky floorboards as she bounced around the bedroom upstairs. There was the splashing in the first floor bathroom, and she was gently humming carols to herself again.

These were ordinary sounds that he was used to, although he was curious about the nature of his gift. It was one that was causing her to practically skip around the guest room.

The peculiarity came, however, when he heard an impossible amount of footsteps and a succession of different giggles. Miriam could be heavy-footed at times and prone to accidents, but she couldn't produce the level of voices that he had heard. She even raced up to their bedroom on the top third floor and started chattering. Almost as if she was talking to someone else. Whenever he queried such sounds, shouting upwards to her to see if she was alright, she called down in response to shush him, telling him that he had to be patient. The unknowing was a tad nauseating. He drowned the uncomfortable feelings with the dregs of his whisky.

When nine had rolled around, and the grandfather clock in the hallway chimed out, Miriam finally beckoned him. "John, will you come to the stairs please?"

"Thank goodness," he muttered to himself as he placed the glass down on the table beside him and walked out of the living room into the hallway. He stood at the bottom of the stairs and looked up to where Miriam was standing.

He was thankful that he had, indeed, discarded the glass because he would've immediately dropped it. Miriam was wearing the most decadent outfit he had ever seen her in. It was practically burlesque. For a start, she was pretty much only wearing underwear. She wore a black lace chemise that sat in the middle of her thick thighs. The top nestled comfortably at her giving cleavage which she had plumped with the corset. Another deliciously devilish garment. It was completely black, from the satin base to the frills of lace across the boning and hems. Over her arms, she wore a silk white floor-length dressing gown. It was as though it were she who reached into the sky and draped the heavens across her. Her brown hair was liberated and cascaded down her body in her signature unkempt waves. Her lips had a dark shade upon them and her navy eyes were incandescent with indecency.

With the curves of her plush body on true display, Miriam looked phenomenal. No. There was no word truly for how exquisite she was right in that moment. He wanted to dive in and take her on the cold wooden floor of their landing.

Finding himself collapsing to his knees on the bottom of the steps, John let out a small groan and laugh of appreciation. From this angle, he was most certain that she was not wearing any drawers. He practically whimpered again with that thought.

"Do you like?" she said, putting a hand upon her hip and the other to the sky, showing how gorgeously the gown draped over her.

"Oh most ardently!" He lifted himself up from the stairs and started to climb them very slowly. She stayed as stationary as a statue as he ascended to her beauty. When he reached the landing, he wound a hand around her waist and brought her body against his so that she could feel how rock-hard he was for her. He growled into her ear, "What beautiful garments for the bedroom floor!"

She smiled at him but did not give away her ploy. Instead, she nodded at the washroom to the left of them. "All in good time John. This is only part of your present." She gestured to the small washroom beside them. "Your outfit is in there. Clean up and look presentable, please."

Very swiftly, he did as he was instructed. He did not want to spend a single second away from her, knowing she was out there, looking as she did. She had prepared a small basin of water with his lavender soap and cloth. He soothed over every inch of his skin, washing away traces of sweat and dirt from the day. He even rubbed his teeth again to refresh his entire body. Then he put on his new outfit. It was not much. Just a fresh white billowy shirt with black trousers and braces. As always, the Bennetts perfectly matched.

Back on the landing, Miriam greeted him with a glass of champagne. She clinked hers against his and bowed her head. She then reached out her hand for him to grab and started to lead them up the last set of stairs to their bedroom.

He freed a breath in an animated fashion.

At last I can finally be inside of my wife.

When they reached the bedroom door, Miriam inhaled as though she were steeling herself. She let go of his hand and met John's eyes with a fierce authoritative look upon her face. "The rule is this, Dr John Bennett, you can only watch. You are not allowed to touch anything, or anyone, or even talk unless I explicitly instruct otherwise. Do you understand?"

John's eyes widened. He nodded in response, fearing her ruling had started immediately.

"Good boy." Miriam let out a peep of excitement. "Now I am afraid your present is as much a gift for myself as it is for you."

She pushed the door of their bedroom open.

And there, sitting on their bed, drinking champagne, were their best friends.

Michael and Adelaide Jenkins.

Chapter Eight:

The Question

It had started off as a question on their wedding day.

This had not been the first time someone had been bold enough to make such an inquiry to Miriam. But usually the question was meant as a jibe. A way of conveying their utmost disapproval. The usual culprits were Aunt Isobel's social "elite," who Miriam loathed for their gossiping ways and lack of action in actual important matters. They always assumed scandal. Either Miriam was pregnant, or her father had insisted on their hasty betrothal to save her from a life of spinsterhood. They would not say such brazen things to her face. No, most were afraid of Miriam's sharp tongue. Instead, they would slyly ask the question in scathing biting tones. Little did they know that she saw through their ruse.

She would answer the same every time. "Perhaps if you had known a smidgeon of love in your life you would understand, rather than spread malicious gossip about people you do not know."

With none of the parasites at the wedding at the Clayton Manor in the countryside, Miriam was surprised to encounter the question though it did not come with the same inflections. In the front room, she sat alone in an armchair, drinking champagne by the fire for a bit of respite from the event's flurry. Hettie and Isobel were playing card games in the dining room. The men were having a cigar in her father's study. Most of the other guests had left by the evening.

She heard tipsy footsteps make their clumsy way down the stairs. Peering out to the hallway, she saw a slightly unstable and confused Adelaide. Miriam giggled and called out, "I am in here my little chuckaboo."

"Oh Miriam, thank goodness." Her American twang was slurred as she made her way to the living room. Several drinks across the course of the day had stripped Adelaide away from all of her quaint graces. Instead, she flopped down on the armchair opposite Miriam's and huffed a little bit. "I fear I may have imbibed far too much today."

"I fear not enough," Miriam said as she reached over to her champagne bottle and poured an extra glass for her new friend. She had only known Adelaide for two weeks, but they were becoming firm favourites of one another. She leaned over to pass the drink which Adelaide took happily, only spilling a small amount on her hand. Miriam pretended not to notice. "It shall be nice to share a drink together without our husbands." She gasped a little, giving a soft smile, and said in a hushed tone, "My goodness, my husband!"

"I do not know why you are so…" Adelaide punctuated, incorrectly, her sentence so that she could down her champagne. She leaned over for Miriam to top her up. "… shocked Miriam. It is as though you have been married for lifetimes."

Miriam grinned and practically glowed. "I feel that way also."

"That is why you were married so soon, is it not?" Adelaide gestured with her glass causing droplets of the liquid to fall on her beloved baby blue ballgown. "Because you are soulmates?"

"How very astute of you Adelaide!" Miriam took her own sip fairly nervously for they were delicately dancing around some of the accusations that had stalked her nuptials. Adelaide's sentence still rang loud, despite how lovingly it was delivered.

"Well, your father is too kind, and you are far too headstrong, for him to cajole you into marriage." Adelaide waved her hand dismissively, addressing the rumours quite perfectly and without hesitation. "And… pfft… You being with child? That seems quite ridiculous even though I know you two have already had relations." The blonde-haired woman slapped her hand across her mouth immediately.

Miriam flipped her head back around to the hallway. She leaned backwards to see if her aunt had heard Adelaide's sudden outburst. When a slight slam against the table and a loud cheer from Hettie rang out, Miriam was satisfied that she was safe. She huffed air out of her nose as she turned back to her friend. "You are fairly candid when you've had a drink Adelaide. Here I thought you were the quiet one."

"Oh I am sorry for being so impertinent."

"How did you know?"

"Frankly, it was a wild guess.. There is no… apprehension between you. Just an absolute adoration. One that comes from knowing the other both in body and soul."

Miriam mused on what Adelaide had said as she sipped gently on her beverage. The bubbles matched those popping within her stomach. She thought on John's gracious nudity and his kind words. How lucky she was to have known these qualities already. "I could not have put it better myself but Adelaide…" She tapped the arm of the chair. "Do you wish to know the real reason why we were wed so soon?"

"Yes." Adelaide giggled. She walked over and sat promptly on where Miriam was tapping.

Miriam wrapped her arm around her friend which caused the tipsy American to fall into her lap. The pair were already tittering. Adelaide wriggled onto Miriam playfully, causing a small buzz across Miriam's privates. She breathed out heavily and scooped her friend's blonde ringlets from her ear. She glanced to make sure nobody had strayed nearby before she murmured, "It is because I could not stand a single day without his cock."

Adelaide honked and wheezed as her cheeks grew red. "You are *awful*, Miriam Clayton. OH, I suppose it is Bennett now." Adelaide did not move from Miriam's lap however, not even when Miriam squeezed against her waist. "If I may be so bold to admit, that in spite of Michael's strict conducts, he too was not virginal when we wed. Not at all virginal…"

"My, that is a surprise. Who knew Michael Jenkins had it in him?"

"You will be amazed by what Michael has in him…"

The men emerged from their smoking session and found the women in fits of uncontrollable giggles.

From that point on, Miriam and Adelaide were firm friends. They saw each other at least twice a week to discuss many things, such as raising funds to build Miriam's dream refuge, any gossip the pair might have had from their respective circles, and, of course, their husbands. Over the course of their friendship, Miriam started to insinuate the idea of tonight. Especially when Adelaide expressed how she longed for adventures.

Adelaide at first dismissed the notion when Miriam planted it into her mind. But like all good ideas, however racy they may be, the seed sprouted. Its roots stretched down and consumed her dreams. Miriam was a good gardener and watered the suggestion until its fruition. During December, she was thrilled to see it bloom and blossom.

It must have taken Adelaide an entire day to convince Michael to join them. Although Miriam knew that Michael could not resist Adelaide's insistence, there was a slight worry that his overtly traditional sensibilities could not be shaken. Of course, she always had a second scheme for her husband if her friends had cold feet. However, the minute she heard the bang from upstairs and saw the fireplace on, she concluded that her plan was in motion. Adelaide and Michael had sneaked in whilst Miriam and John were at dinner. Still, she rushed up to whisper to her best friend through the bedroom door to triple check they were there.

Miriam did not focus on the couple who were on the bed, tipsy and giggly. Instead, she studied the look on her husband's face and tried to stop the corners of her mouth twitching. He even took a step back, completely shocked at the scene in front of him. He gripped his glass, rubbing against it so tightly that it produced a small squeak. He opened his mouth slightly as if he were to say something, but he did not dare to. After all, that would be breaking her explicit instructions.

When a minute had passed, John gave a small nod of agreement. Miriam swore she saw a flicker of a smile underneath that dumbfounded expression. She once again weaved her fingers into his free hand and pulled him into the bedroom, causing the door to close behind them with a slight bang and click. There was no turning back now. They were past the point of no return.

"Good evening John," Adelaide said as she raised a glass to him. She then emitted a nervous honk of her loud laugh. "Forgive the intrusion."

John could not respond. Instead, he nodded his welcome. First to Adelaide, and then again to his friend who tipped a nervous glass back. There was a flush on Michael's face that Miriam relished. It was a mixture of intoxication and apprehension. For once he was quiet and in her domain. She fluttered him a wink which further increased the volume of red on his cheeks. The feeling was unparalleled, having two men in a fluster. Even Adelaide seemed unsure of how the night was going to go as Miriam assumed all control.

She was, however, always a perfect hostess. Adelaide had followed her instructions to a tee. The fireplace in their bedroom was smouldering whilst there were many candles and lamps dotted around the room. The red decorated room was drenched in a hellfire. There were two bottles of champagne in a bucket on Miriam's dresser whilst Michael and Adelaide drank from an open one that sat on the bedside cabinet. A chair had been placed facing the end of the bed.

The Jenkins had already absconded with their shoes, their coats, and Michael's burgundy jacket. Adelaide, surprisingly, wore a darker blue than she usually did. The evening dress had merely thin straps so that she showed off her neckline and cleavage. Her blonde hair was tightly ringleted and fell just beneath her chin. Miriam could not wait to see and touch as much as possible.

She walked her husband across their bedroom as though he had never entered there. John squeezed her hand for comfort to which she squeezed back. It was a signal to tell him that all was going to be alright. Miriam placed him on the chair. She sauntered over to the open bottle and poured him a fresh glass, leaving the remains of the champagne beside his feet so that he could indulge when needed. And boy, he would need to. He breathed out and took a small sip. "Remember the rules darling. You are not allowed to touch anything, or anyone, or even talk unless I explicitly instruct otherwise."

A fear and an excitement flew through his icy eyes.

She kissed him gently on the cheek as his small reward for being so obedient. Then she spun slowly around to the eager couple on the bed. All the while she slipped her white silk dressing gown from her person, a gentle swoosh silencing nearly everyone. Scantily clad, Miriam placed her hands on her hips as three sets of eyes clamoured over her.

There was no power quite like this.

As one would addressing a big audience, Miriam extended her hands and said, "Now, shall we begin?"

Chapter Ten:

The Festivities

"Good Heavens Miriam, you look sensational."

Adelaide's face was almost the same colour as the walls of the bedroom, but her eyes remained unblinking, slinking across Miriam's form.

"Thank you ever so much, my little chuckaboo."

Miriam's first act was one that she had been dying to do ever since Michael Jenkins first walked his wife into last year's hospital Christmas party. She leaned down slowly and dragged a finger down Adelaide's sharp jaw, causing the woman to giggle nervously. When Miriam reached Adelaide's chin, she pushed it upwards so that their mouths were very close. Adelaide's breathing halted. Miriam stopped because she wanted to tease but also because she needed permission, as she flicked her eyes upwards to Adelaide. There was the added reward of taunting her ensnared silent husband as she revealed her wanting, wet cunt whilst bent over. When she heard the chair squeak as he shuffled, she knew that she was successful.

Adelaide inhaled and nodded her permission. Miriam pressed her mouth against her friend's and moaned immediately. Adelaide was soft and tasted like wine. The American had never kissed a woman before. In fact, had never kissed anyone except her two husbands, having been married and widowed before Michael. So she was hesitant at first but still she placed her hand upon Miriam's face and soon matched the movements.

When they parted, Adelaide giggled, and her face was almost beetroot. Miriam turned her attention to Michael who was surprisingly mute as he watched, wide-eyed, the scene in front of him. He clung on to his glass for dear life - practically shaking like a reprimanded up pup. She couldn't quite discern his emotions and whether he was completely ready for what was about to unfold. Michael Jenkins irritated Miriam, a lot, and they butted heads over a lot of issues in the hospital boardroom. Thanks to her friendship with Adelaide, however, she was starting to find a fondness for him. He cared very deeply and very lovingly about his wife. Something that Miriam could support.

And besides, what frustration could not be solved with some light fucking?

Miriam grinned broadly. "Adelaide, may I kiss your husband?"

"You may," Adelaide replied as she leaned back and drank champagne to watch.

As Miriam approached Michael, he unfroze and started to stammer, "Now, Miriam, if I may… can I just say before anything happens and we do anything rash that I wish for you to know… for you to all know… well I am inclined to mention that I—"

"Let us find a better use for that mouth, Jenkins."

Miriam kissed him with a little bit more force than she had Adelaide. She shoved her tongue fully into his mouth as though that were the only way she could silence him – by stealing all the words he was about to say. He was frozen at first but soon she found him wiggling against her as a hot breath left his nose.

Afterwards, he was completely stunned.

Miriam smiled more sweetly this time, rather than the hungry animal that she was. She knew that he was nervous. Both of the Jenkins were. They had wandered into a lion's enclosure. Miriam delicately caressed Michael's cheek to soothe away any nerves that he was having. "Michael, I understand this is very new and very scary, but I wish to take care of you and your wife and all your needs." She sat back so that she could see Adelaide and address them both. "Whatever happens in this bedroom, stays here. A secret between us and the wallpaper. We can resume our usual loathing of one another the moment you leave." She fluttered them both a small wink which caused Adelaide to titter more. "And if at any time you feel unsafe or uncertain, then you must say a completely unusual word that'll stop the action. For myself and John…" Finally, she turned around to look at her husband. He was as still as a statue with a sparkle of sin in his stare. She smiled and turned slowly back to the Jenkins' on the bed "… it is roses. Now, what would you like?"

Adelaide thought hard with a tuneful hum. "Perhaps, ours could be 'New Year's' darling, what do you think?"

"Y-yes." Michael nodded slightly confused as he reached out a hand to his wife and threaded her fingers into hers. Adelaide leaned over and kissed him to show that no matter what happened next, it would not change their relationship. If anything, it could bring them closer in passion.

Miriam rolled her tongue across the back of her teeth, eager to dive in and join them. "A very good word, indeed, Adelaide. Good girl."

"Oh!" Adelaide grinned as she peeled herself away from her husband's lips. "Oh, I like that very much, Miriam." A thrill shimmered through her hazel eyes as though she finally felt safe to awaken all of her desire. She placed her empty glass of champagne on John's bedside cabinet on the left of the bed. "I suddenly feel very overdressed."

"How fortuitous! I too was about to make the same observation. Allow me."

Miriam wasted little time. She needed to see her friend's naked body immediately. She kissed Adelaide again. This time the pair did not hesitate. They were clearly both hungry for this as they groaned against one another. Miriam skimmed the straps over Adelaide's shoulder. Snaking her hands around the back of the slight woman's body, Miriam pressed against Adelaide. All the while, her hand's found the tiny metal clasps and wriggled them free. They parted from kissing so Miriam could peel the full dress from Adelaide. As it fell to the floor, there was no stopping Miriam. She could not be steady, not when she needed to see her best friend's entire form. She clawed at the corset, dragged down the drawers, and lifted the chemise until Adelaide was finally naked.

Adelaide lay back on her elbows and allowed Miriam to observe her. It was amusing how her friend paralleled her husband so remarkably. They were both more reserved than Michael and Miriam in social settings and could be happy in silence, though Adelaide, at times, had a fondness for gossip and a audacious tongue after alcohol. In the bedroom, they both exuded extreme confidence. Adelaide must've known that her body was beautiful. From her small pert breasts to her toned stomach to the curl of blonde on her mound.

Dragging a finger across her friend's supple skin, Miriam glanced over to her husband to see his reaction. Almost as though she was exhibiting her latest find. John had not moved much since the last time she glanced over though his wine had almost gone. His mouth, however, was slightly open. She ruminated on how hard he was right now as their eyes caught for a second, sharing the same thought.

"I think my husband and I both agree that you are simply heavenly."

Miriam kissed the woman before she turned her attention to Michael. She took the champagne flute from his hand and placed it on her dresser behind him. This time she took it slow. He breathed raggedly as she unbuttoned his wine red waistcoat and unravelled his bowtie. She fiddled with his shirt and tie. Then she wiggled him from his vest, freed him from his trousers, and his drawers. All the while she gave him pecks on his lips to show him that this was more than fine.

He was shyer than his wife when Miriam scrutinised him. His whole skin flushed the same colour as his suit. He had a lanky and skinny tall frame. There were small patches of light blonde curls like Adelaide's across his chest and a darker set on his privates. His penis, which was currently semi-hard at the moment, was not too bad at all. There was an attractiveness to him, however, that she could not deny.

Besides, Miriam admired the naked form of anyone. She could easily be turned on by all shapes and sizes. She admired plump fat bodies and squishy bellies and wonky breasts and skinny legs and stubby penises and large vulvas and hairy women and short men. Dark skin, pale skin, and freckled skin, she found that anyone could be beautiful splayed out upon her bed, demanding to be pleasured by her.

Of course, in all of her sexual adventures, there was nobody quite as divine as her husband.

With both of The Jenkins now undressed and lying side by side, Miriam could no longer stand being clothed. She wiggled slightly so her husband could only see her back. She removed her corset and chemise with ease. There was a chorus of gasps.

Suddenly there was a clinking of glass on glass. She twisted her head about to see her husband pouring himself more champagne. He looked up at her with his dazzling blue eyes as he placed the bottle back down and crossed his legs. He had an expression that one would have at a theatre show, watching an intriguing play that he could dissect. Then he slyly gestured at her to proceed with a rolling wave of his hand.

She squeaked and beamed. Not that she needed his permission, but she was happy he seemed to be enjoying himself. There was no sign of their safe word anywhere. She turned back to the couple beneath her. She leaned down to kiss Adelaide again, wanting to feel how well their nudeness felt pressed against one another. "Michael," Miriam whispered whilst her cheek leaned against Adelaide. "Michael, I am going to pleasure your wife now. Unlike my husband, you can touch yourself if you so desire. I suggest you take notes."

Adelaide let out a gasp at this as Miriam pushed her down on the bed. She grabbed hold of Adelaide's knees and spread them apart for easy access. Then she made her way down to Adelaide's notch hearing a gentle sigh come from her friend. Miriam first skimmed her fingertips across the slit which was already glistening. Then she pushed into her nether lips, causing Adelaide to whine. She looked up to see Adelaide gazing at the ceiling as she bit her lip. Michael was lazily cupping himself.

Miriam's fingers swiped up and down, spreading the wetness across Adelaide's madge so that she could get more gratification. Then Miriam settled on Adelaide's clitoris. She began to circle it deftly, causing a delightfully musical selection of sighs to leave her friend's mouth.

But Miriam was hankering for a taste. She bent down to slide her tongue across Adelaide's wetness. Adelaide bucked and cried out. Her hand slapped over and grabbed her husband's arm, giving it a squeeze. Adelaide tasted great – a mixture of sweet and sour as Miriam lapped up the moistness. She flicked her tongue against her friend's sensitive spot and drove two fingers into her opening. Adelaide gave an enormous whine and begged Miriam not to stop. Miriam curled her fingers inside and started pushing. The sounds Adelaide were making were a symphony. Suddenly they were stifled. Miriam flicked her eyes upwards and saw that Adelaide had wrapped a hand around Michael's neck and pulled him down so he could kiss her fervently. His hand moved up and down his member still.

It made Miriam work harder. She wanted to see Adelaide come undone and shake in her husband's arms. Miriam's fingers pushed in with greater force.

With her other hand, Miriam skirted down to her own vagina and began to play. She was bent down in the mesh of Adelaide's privates, but she had her buttocks raised so John could at least see how dripping she was.

Suddenly, Adelaide clamped her thighs around Miriam's face as her insides contracted. She parted from Michael's lips and almost screamed with climax. Miriam helped Adelaide ride the wave, coaxing as much elation from the women as possible before she slackened and stopped.

Adelaide flopped back on her back and breathed intensely.

Miriam sat up, dancing her coated fingertips into her mouth. She then wagged one at Adelaide and smiled. "I am not entirely done with you yet Adelaide."

"What? But Miriam I just—OH!!"

But Miriam interrupted her by scooping her tiny body and placing it in the lap of Michael. She manoeuvred them so that John could see everyone a little bit better. She did not want him to miss any of this. "There, hold onto your wife Michael and watch how quickly I can make her climax again."

Miriam pressed her hands on Adelaide's knees to keep them spread so that they could press their slits close together. As Miriam mounted her friend, she thought about how this all came to fruition. How the four of them had ended up in this licentious performance. And how a nice societal lady like Adelaide Jenkins found herself writhing naked below the hot-headed Miriam Bennett.

It would shock most men to learn how foul their wife's mouths and minds could be. Of course, not every woman would be so forthcoming with their sexual attractions and need for pleasures. Some would scold it just as much as their patriarchal brethren and would rather curtail to some bizarre, restricted construct rather than just be themselves.

Women in their society *had* to be demure, did they not?

They could not show an ounce of passion to the outside world, lest they lock them up for hysterics or condemn them to spinsterhood. That was not Doctor Miriam Bennett at all. Miriam went against the grain of her standing, finding solace with a wave of new century women who fought for intellect and the right for autonomy. She really liked sex and pleasure and domination and sought it out whenever she could, finding a kindred spirit with her husband John.

Adelaide had the air of a wealthy creature. She would attend functions with older ladies and titled people. She would crochet and knit and sew and work on her charity ventures. But as she grew closer to Miriam, she felt freer to express that there was something rakish nestled in the core of her spirit.

For Miriam, she had always had an attraction to Adelaide and had dreamed of what sex with her would feel like. For Adelaide, she had always promised herself adventure after a cold marriage left her widowed. However, she had unwillingly fallen for Michael and found herself wedded again. She wanted to explore, and Miriam was already an experienced voyager.

So as Miriam began to rock gently against Adelaide, she was pleased she could accommodate another's dark desires. After all, she had a wonderful talent in bringing it to fruition. Besides, the minute her cunt met Adelaide's, she realised how truly throbbing and aching she was for this. It probably wasn't going to take very long.

Still she moved upon her friend and was surprised when Adelaide began to match the rhythm. Adelaide reached one hand around her husband whilst she placed another on Miriam's thigh. A ripple of sensations spread through Miriam, and a light whimper escaped from her.

There was another shuffling next to them. Miriam flicked her attention to John to see him trying to adjust without touching his crotch. He had uncrossed his legs and pulled at his trousers by his knee. He must be throbbing - his prick painful in its confines. He let out a frustrated sigh – the loudest he had been since he entered the room.

Realising this made Miriam gyrate against Adelaide with a sudden need. Adelaide began to whine again, indecipherable words emanating from her lips as she couldn't believe she was about to climax again. Miriam reached a hand down and grabbed one of Adelaide's breasts, squeezing it to help spur on both of their arrivals. It took a few more moments as they slipped and slid against one another before Adelaide spluttered out, "Oh my LORD, Miriam. I am…"

Adelaide interrupted herself with her own orgasm in a heavy cry. She twisted against Michael's body as he kissed her. As she twitched alongside Miriam's wetness, Miriam found herself also near completion. She gripped onto Adelaide's waist as she quickened - excited when an orgasm shuddered through her as well. She held onto Adelaide tightly as she threw her head back and cried loudly, the electricity plummeting through her body fast and plentifully.

She tried not to collapse but started to slow down as the pleasure pirouetted around her. In a haze of satisfaction, she smiled and untangled herself from her friend. "Outstanding, Adelaide, truly remarkable."

But Miriam didn't stop. If anything, her first orgasm of the day bristled in her, and called to all the other cells in her body to come alive. She scrabbled off of a very tired Adelaide and let her friend rest for a little while before she turned to Michael. "And now it is your turn."

She swore she saw Michael gulp. His dick was very hard from witnessing such a scene. She kissed him and fondled his cock to show how serious she was. Then she positioned herself on all fours at the end of the bed so that she could face her own husband. John had been sipping on some wine but froze immediately when he realised what was happening. A quake of uncertainty rocked between them. Had Miriam pushed them too far? She couldn't be sure, but it was too late to go back.

Michael scrambled and was soon behind her. There was another hesitant beat as he breathed out. Miriam turned around and nodded at him, so he slid inside. They both gasped with the same inflection. After all, if you had ever witnessed their sparring matches at work, you would be surprised to see them in such a configuration. Perhaps there was merit in the saying, "there is a fine line between love and hate." Miriam flicked her eyes to Adelaide who crouched on her knees beside them. A lopsided grin formed on the blonde American as her hand started to lazily play below again. She even kissed her husband as he fucked another to prove how much she was appreciating this scene.

As Michael took hold of her hips, his fingers plunging into her plentiful flesh, he began thrusting into Miriam. She gripped the end of the bed. There was some skill here in the rhythm. He was not completely useless as she had assumed. After all, he had only one experience and that was with Adelaide. Still, he moved within Miriam at a good pace, striking something within her that caused her moan and pant.

"Not bad, Michael, not bad at all."

She kept her eyes fixated on her husband as his blue eyes blazed. What was he feeling at this moment? Many men could dismiss women fucking women as nothing more than their titillation for their own amusement. But letting another man enter her so soon into their marriage? That was a curious boundary to have crossed already. Still, John did not say anything. He did not do anything. He merely watched with no clear countenance upon his face, observing silently as his best friend drove into his wife. Somehow, this whole act made Miriam appreciate her husband even more and she started to truly revel in the act she was committing.

Suddenly, John leaned forward. He dared not touch her, but his lips skimmed the air by her cheek, and his breath fell upon her skin. Nestling next to her ear, with a devilish tone, he whispered, "Does he fuck you better than I?"

When he sat back down, Miriam lost control, and she fell to her elbows. Those words precariously slipped down her entire body. She was afraid of coming undone too soon because of his petulance. Looking back up, John tipped his glass to her with a flicker of a sly smirk. She gasped and groaned, thinking only on how he could pleasure her better than anyone in this entire world.

The answer was no.

It was absolutely no.

But she would not give in that easily.

After all, he had crossed the line.

Miriam shook her head and moved back to her hands. She called out to her friend. "Adelaide, my husband broke the rules…" She met her husband's fervid stare. "He deserves to be punished."

Chapter Nine:

The Angel

Oh no.

John thought to himself as the words fell around him. He knew that crossing the line would incur punishment, but he assumed that would come later. He did not grasp that Miriam was sly enough to concoct something there and then. When Adelaide's smile mirrored the same diabolic grin on his wife's face, he realised that not only was he about to be pulled into the scene before him, but his deepest secret was about to be revealed.

As Adelaide skirted off the bed, John's mind raced. He had liked immensely the show that Miriam had put on for him this evening. The way she undressed Michael and Adelaide and then herself. The way she showed him how salivating she was when she brought Adelaide to fruition. The way the two women coiled and cried out together was more tormenting than ever.

The way she was taken by Michael had even rocked through – a tortuous stab of jealousy and tantalisation that was more intoxicating than the champagne. He could not deny that soaked in mortification and anticipation, trapped under her rulings, he was more stimulated than he had ever been. His prick was so very achingly hard, wishing to be involved somehow. Yet having to obey her was making his head dizzy.

He did not know what was going to happen next.

So he was shocked when Adelaide took his glass and placed it on the floor. He was surprised when she pulled him from his chair. He was amazed when she started to remove his clothes. He was alarmed and aroused. All the while he looked at Miriam. He needed permission to join in. She winked at him, and he pointedly gaped at Adelaide's pert breasts.

Whilst John had bedded only a small variety of women in his lifetime, he truly worshipped the female form - whether that was curvy or slight or even rotund. Their breasts and their notches were, indeed, also helpful when spurring attraction within him. He could not trace his fancies to one dominant feature. He just felt moved by a woman and her luscious body.

None had moved him quite as well as his wife's did.

Now, she had gifted him her very best friend. He felt Adelaide's eyes glance over his nude form and felt weak with lust. She turned back Miriam as though she were giving enthusiastic approval. Miriam smiled, not shaking in her dominant aura, even as Michael moved within her. Perhaps she too was feeling a stab of jealousy now that John was nude and about to do unspeakable things to another woman.

But Miriam had a dastardly plan. Adelaide led John to the bed and bent him over. He settled his hands next to his wife - so close that her panting breaths landed upon his cheek. She glanced up to Adelaide and nodded. Suddenly a hand struck John's behind. He bellowed more out of shock than pain, though his arse cheeks were still sore from his earlier beating. Adelaide smacked him again and he turned his attention to his wife. How much had she told her best friend about his secret needs and wants? Enough for Adelaide to understand this punishment? Or perhaps she was just following orders with no understanding of what she was doing?

Miriam replied by, at last, kissing him. A reward for his punishment. Whenever there was a slap, there was another kiss. It moved like this for a few minutes. John's buttocks were almost raw after Adelaide had begun hitting him hard. The slick droplets of shame slithered into his stomach at having his friends witness such an act. The humiliation only fanned the flames of lust.

Suddenly, Michael groaned and moved faster, clinging eagerly onto Miriam's hips. She laughed in response. "Oh oh oh ah, no, not yet Michael, I want you to see my husband fuck your wife."

With that clear cue, Adelaide halted spanking John. Instead, she crawled onto the bed next to him on all fours and wriggled her permissions. John hesitated and looked to his wife. She winked and said, "Merry Christmas, darling."

He could not help but grin as he stationed himself behind Adelaide. She reached behind herself and gripped his thick member, her slight hands making him feel bigger. Guiding him to her entrance, John took a deep breath before he slid into another. Someone who was not Miriam. It was a strange sensation. After all, he was so used to his wife. He had practically memorised every inch of her. But Adelaide was snug and warm. It was strange but not dreadful.

He began moving, bucking his dick into her tight channel. Adelaide gasped and John swore she glanced at Miriam with an approving smile. John climbed onto the bed so that he and Adelaide were a perfect mirror of Michael and Miriam. He gripped onto the slender woman's hips and began prodding at a greater rate. He had a lot of pent up emotions thanks to the whole day of tantalising teasing.

Plus, he would be the first to admit that this was a rather strange outcome for the night. There he was ploughing into his best friend's wife whilst his best friend did the same to his own wife. It did not seem odd to both the women about this strange equation, but John had tried his best to not make eye contact with Michael, fearing that it may be too awkward to do so. However, there was a small moment in the middle of this act where Michael and John shared a passing glance. One of equal bemusement and almost a glimmer of approval from Jenkins with an almost grin.

John peered down to watch his friend move. Michael exerted his breathing as though this were merely exercise and puffed out in rhythm. Sweat glistened over his friend's svelte body and he could see muscles appear in his arms with each momentum.

John felt his cheeks redden.

He looked away and moved his eyeline to his wife whose deep blue eyes watched him intently, dazzling with depravity as her mouth widened with wickedness.

"Adelaide, would you like my husband to bring you to climax?"

"I… I… I would very much like that."

John nodded to Miriam. He reached down to Adelaide's already well-worked clit and started playing. She practically trembled when he did. John was very adept at this skill. His fingers moved in different motions. At first he circled gently, then he would rub in perpendicular motions, then he would pinch slightly. He did this in different cycles, moving at unique speeds, and pressures. All the while his cock slammed into her, faster and deeper. It wasn't long before Adelaide's insides contracted around his dick, wetting him as she noisily came. She tried to keep steady as he still moved but Adelaide was quaking whilst her hands gripped the bedsheets.

Miriam showed her approval. "Very good Adelaide."

Michael was next to follow. He gripped onto Miriam's hips again and moved at great speed, letting out a whimper. She wouldn't stop him this time, not when they were all close to finishing. Instead she encouraged him to furiously fuck her harder, gasping as he took her repeatedly. John's eyes stayed fixed on Miriam's during this action. Her smile was unruly.

"Wait, Michael… I want to see how your face looks." Miriam pushed him out of her and flipped over onto her back. She sneakily threw her hand back and grabbed John's calf. "You can release yourself on me."

It did not take long for it to happen. Michael had been on the edge for a while. With just a few slight pumps of his cock, he grimaced and ejaculated onto Miriam, spraying first her hairy mound and then upwards onto her belly. He grunted and groaned as he spurted what he could. She preened happily before he too collapsed backwards onto the pillows.

"Excellent work Michael."

John continued thrusting into Adelaide but watched with unsure emotions unfurling. He was embarrassed that he had seen his best friend undone in such a manner, exhilarated by the same notion in equal measure, and maybe just a bit enraged that someone else had coated his wife with their ejaculate. He pounded into Adelaide harder and faster than ever. Adelaide cried out and arched her back as he grabbed her forearms, pulled them behind her and held on tightly.

Miriam dipped a finger into the semen and gazed upwards at her husband and placed it into her mouth, sucking slowly as if it were a sweet. John groaned loudly as he continued his fast fucking into Adelaide. He was sure enough about to come too as a tightening gripped his balls. Miriam knew it also.

"John… I want your seed as well," Miriam said huskily before she opened her mouth wide. There was no time to nod. He pulled himself out of Adelaide who collapsed on the bed and rushed over to his wife. He shoved his dick into her mouth and discharged as she sucked onto him. When every bit of his lust had spilled down her throat, John too fell onto the bed in a wave of exhaustion, leaning against the frame.

The only person who did not seem tired was Miriam. She sprung up and watched the spent trio around her with a grin so wide it was as though she swallowed a crescent moon. First, she kissed Michael, then Adelaide, before she finally kissed John. Deeper than the rest as she melted her adoration into his lips.

"Well, you all certainly came in and got to know me better."

The four of them fell into fits of laughter.

It wasn't long before a silence grew in the room. Both Miriam and John noticed a growing hesitation from Michael and Adelaide. They had large smiles on their faces and were satisfied, but suddenly their sensibilities were creeping back. As though they were becoming shameful of their bodies once more. Miriam threw a small look to John upon this realisation. She was a fine hostess, indeed, but she thrived in the aftercare.

After a few minutes immersed in their naked entangled mess, she unfurled herself from their bodies and started to scoot around the bedroom. She found Adelaide's chemise first and gently placed it over the small blonde-haired woman's body. She then found Michael's trousers and his shirt and turned her back whilst he stood up and put them on his body. When he flopped down on the bed, gasping a little as though he had exerted himself too much, Miriam found him a glass of champagne and encouraged him to drink. As a kindness, she kissed him on the cheek and whispered, "Are you alright Michael?"

"Yes," he said but that was all he could muster. His eyes were heavy and staring.

Adelaide was also handed another glass of champagne as she wriggled her corset on. She was asked the same question and replied with a broad smile.

Miriam found her and John's dressing gowns. As he wrapped himself up in his own, he watched his wife don her silk white garment. Stretching her arms up, it looked as though she were unfurling her angel wings. She climbed back onto bed with him, lying opposite one another as their friends gradually found the rest of their belongings and dressed fully. They were tipsy and fumbled and giggled and sighed aplenty. Miriam focused on her husband as he smiled brightly at her. There was no sense of exhaustion within him. Not yet anyway. It was almost as though they were both waiting to be alone.

The Jenkins were dressed and ready to go. Michael merely nodded his goodbyes. Before they parted, Adelaide kissed Miriam one final time – deeply -- and squeezed her hand. "Thank you, Miriam. Truly."

And then The Jenkins left the bedroom for good.

Chapter Ten:

The Bennetts

The front door of the Bennett household closed shut.

The soft knock and click reverberated upwards, and an immediate silence skulked into the room. Though it was not quite quiet in their minds. The evening's activities were noisy, as they echoed across the early hours of the morning. The sounds of sweet sex like a stunning symphony that Miriam had conducted to a climatic crescendo. Now those notes melded into memories. Alone again in their vulgar little bedroom, The Bennetts lay on their sides facing one another. As Miriam caught John's eye, they both burst into uncontrollable laughter.

After a short while, their giggling subsided and they both mused on the day. They were tired and spent but they did not want to fall asleep. Not just yet. Not when they could shift into their timeless space and reflect on the magic of their coupling. Miriam interlocked her fingers with John's. He held onto her tightly, giving her a little squeeze, before he kissed the back of her hand. He sighed deeply. "You are remarkable."

"You flatter me." She bristled a little as her cheeks flushed.

"If anything my darling girl, I have understated. There are no words for how exquisite a creature you are."

He meant it. Over the course of the day, he had seen the very best of his wife. The way she had imparted such decadent rulings. The way she gave passionately to others and felt deeply when another was hurting. The way in which she had understood his trauma and comforted him with her kindness. The way she had welcomed him into her family with fierce devotion. The way she pulled into his darkest of desires and brought them to fruition.

Doctor Miriam Bennett.

What bliss it was to share this world with her.

"It is funny John," she replied in a hushed, revered manner. "I feel the exact same way about you. Words pale in comparison to the perfection that is you."

She meant it also. Over the course of the day she had seen the very best of her husband. The obedience he displayed under her lewd commands. The generosity he had given to people at the hospital. The comfort he had provided when she was sad. The bittersweetness he had showed at her father's house; unafraid to shed a few tears when he finally realised he belonged somewhere.

Doctor John Bennett.

How sweet life was to bring her this gift.

As she felt tears rise in her eyes, John kissed her with all the love he could muster, causing a few to escape. To shed the sadness, Miriam let out a small titter. "To answer your previous question, no. Absolutely not. How could Michael ever compare to you?" She kissed him gently on the lips before she raised an eyebrow. "Adelaide on the other hand…"

He laughed and nudged her playfully.

Rolling onto his back, he reached for two glasses of almost discarded champagne. He wasn't entirely sure who had been drinking from what, but after tonight's activities, it did not matter. He just needed a celebration - to mark the truly remarkable Christmas they had had together. As he passed a glass over to Miriam and they clinked them together immediately.

"John?" she said, stretching out his name in a curious tone so that it became a question.

"Yes Miriam."

"I know we gifted you the brand new candle today as a way of noting new beginnings."

"Indeed you did," he crinkled out a smile and felt a rush of emotions rise to the surface. "It was a great kindness."

Miriam fiddled with the rim of the champagne flute and kept her eyeline low. "I venture that you might wish to light the last bit of the old candle. Would you like to do so now, with me? As a way of remembering your parents. To say goodbye to your old life and all its pains." There was a beat of silence and Miriam's pulse leapt to the throat. She snapped her face up to meet his eyes. "Forgive me if that was impudent. I would also understand if you wished to cherish the last remains. That is also acceptable."

John leaned over and kissed her intensely, caring not for the spilled wine on their bedsheets. Yet again his brilliant wife had reached into his heart and understood him entirely and empathically. She knew every single fibre of his being, right down to the mere morsels. Every day it was as though he was being seen in a manner that he thought only reserved for his own reflection.

He kissed her again because he did not know the words to properly express this. He hoped that the sentence clung to his lips. He wished that the truth hung to his taste. He dreamed that all the words he failed to say slid into her mouth with his tongue.

When they broke for air, he leaned his head against hers. "That sounds like a perfect idea."

He sat up and reached into his bedside drawer, removing the last stub of his childhood candle. Usurping another from its holder, he placed the smudge of wax in and lit the remains

Together they watched the flame as it struggled and cloyed onto the frayed blackened wick.

Miriam watched the fire with great intent, snaking her arm around his as she leaned on his shoulder. In the small glow, she made a small prayer. At first, for the family she saw in the hospital courtyard, hoping they would find solace. Then for her father and her aunt. She even thought about her mother and pictured her watching Miriam grow and could see how blessed she was. She had enough devotion for a thousand lifetimes. She nestled against him, allowing his calming scent to wash over her, and finally made a prayer in thanks for him.

John did, indeed, think of his parents. He wondered if they were watching him and if they were proud of all he had achieved. He had raised himself from ashes, had established a fine career, and now had married the love of his life. Just as they had done. As he watched the small flame flicker, he even thought of his evil aunt. How surprised she would be to find he married a woman of status but God, she would have loathed Miriam. He even pictured how they would spar. But most importantly, he thought about Miriam.

As she nuzzled up beside him, he was overcome with the warmth of her. He needed her in so many different ways. Most strongly, he needed to show her how much she meant to him. "Please, may I finally take you?"

She wanted to more than anything but of course, she would not make it easy on him. She brushed away whatever tears had dared to drag themselves down. Instead of giving him permission, she giggled. "Do you really wish to after another has released himself all over me?"

"Oh yes, you are right," John replied and frowned as though he were trying to solve an enormous puzzle. After a few beats, he then exclaimed loudly, pointing a finger into the air. "I know just the thing."

Without giving her any explanation, he pushed her down so that she lay back against the bed. Shifting between her legs, John fiddled with the rope tie of her dressing gown before he undid the garment, pulled it open, dragged it off her arms, and revealed her naked body to him. He then removed and tossed his own dressing gown across the room.

Immediately, Miriam could see how stiff and craving he was. His eyes were alight with a mischievous flame that dazzled within those bright blues. She tilted her head. "What on earth are you doing?"

John did not answer straight away. Instead, he leaned down and kissed her, twisting his tongue into her mouth as the tip of his erection brushed up against his body. He then leaned down to her ear and whispered darkly. "I am cleaning you up."

Suddenly, he trailed down her body with his mouth. He started first by nestling into her neck, nibbling a little on her earlobe. The tingles shot down into her stomach in the most pleasing way. She gasped, surprised that her body was coming alive again with the way he moved across her. As he dragged his tongue over her chest before placing one of her breasts into his mouth. He sucked on the nipple and squeezed the other breast, causing her to moan loudly. Then he trailed his mouth further down…

"Oh God, John…"

When he had reached her belly, the first place that had the remnants of Michael's climax, he snapped up to look at her. There was a flash of an insolent smile. Then he unfurled his tongue and bent down, scooping up the residue. The sound that escaped Miriam's mouth was indecipherable. As John's tongue slid across her body, using the appendage to eliminate whatever was left of Michael, Miriam bristled with delight. Especially when her husband's mouth moved between her legs.

John let out a groan as he slipped his tongue through her folds. The taste of her was different, the usual tang was mixed with the saltiness of semen and another woman's wetness. She was practically soaking as he dragged himself among the whole of her privates. After a few plentiful lashings, he settled on her sensitive spot and suckled. She cried out loud as she twitched against him.

The whole act was absurdly debauched. He was pleasing her with generous alternating strokes. Miriam did not hold back her giddy sounds as she bucked against him. This was a surprising turn of events: She had barely even had the idea before John had started this act – cleaning another's cream from her body. What man would ever willingly do this? She was reminded on how paired their spirits were – how his own darkness matched the nature within her. And oh how he was so willing to give himself over to her.

Suddenly, and unexpectedly, an orgasm washed over her.

Miriam could not help it. She practically screamed his name as the pleasure took hold. She arched her back and one of her hands into his hair and gripped tightly. The feeling was thunderous and powerful, almost as though it were the very first time that she had orgasmed. He kept on moving his mouth against her, flicking her clitoris with his tongue until she stopped.

When she let go of his hair, John let out a low chuckle. "That was shockingly fast."

"Hmmm." She placed a hand on her chest as though she could calm down her heartbeat as it thudded plentifully and in an almost aching manner. She did not address her quick rise to climax, though it had certainly surprised her as well. Instead, she huffed and cocked a smile. "How did I taste?"

"Why not see for yourself?"

He bent down and pressed his lips against hers. It was a strange combination of flavours as he slid into her mouth. She felt his hard dick brush against her thigh and could immediately feel how wanting he was as it practically pulsed to be inside of her.

When they parted, she answered his wordless turgid needs. "John, you may take me now."

"Thank goodness."

John reached down and placed the head of his cock against her opening. He paused briefly then giggled. "I shall now place my white staff into your cloven inlet."

"Oh yes, Mr Bennett," she replied with a snort.

Without further hesitation, he glided into her slowly causing her to murmur. As much as she had fun teasing him – teasing them both - by denying him this bliss, she enjoyed the feel of him inside of her more than anything in this world. When he started thrusting, steadily, she felt silly for keeping him apart from her for the entirety of the day. She wrapped her legs around his buttocks and helped push forward the deliberate movements.

The way Miriam enveloped him was unparalleled. He would be foolish to say that he didn't care for their previous tryst with their friends, but there was nothing that could compare to his wife. All the quirky little ways in which she provoked him, making him tense. The plump gorgeousness of her body. The tightness as she squeezed him. They were so perfect for one another that his heart swelled. He leaned his head against hers. He did not wish to fuck her. He wanted to make love to her. Gradual, gentle, gratifying love.

The sex was needed for both of them. Yet they were both tired. Very tired. Already spent from their busy evening and the emotions of the day. He winced and huffed as he tried to keep a smooth rhythm. She decided to roll them both over to make it easier. Now with both of them lying on the side, her leg across his, it was easier to be lazy. Besides, she wanted as much of him against her as possible. She pressed her entire body into him as drove up inside of her.

She placed a hand upon his cheek and stared into his eyes as though she were reaching into his soul and soothing all his aches. She smiled and said upon heated breaths, "I love you."

He trembled a little as those words descended around him. Miriam did not say those words often. He knew the depths of her devotion in other ways, but it always filled him with absolution whenever she told him how much she idolised him. He found himself pushing into her with more vigour, keen to spread as much of his own worship into her. It was not long before he finally ejaculated. He let out a small whine of appreciation and leaned his head against hers. "I love you too."

By now they were exhausted, spent in so many different ways. Flickering like the last flame of an old candle. They stayed embroiled in one another, tangled in the heated moments of their devoutness; their bodies pulsating with pleasure. Their breaths slipping out in deep rhythmic beats. Their hearts drumming deeply as one. They fell asleep like this, clinging onto the other with a cloying desperation. A wish that they could remain forever exactly like this. A hope to slip into their cherished timeless space and never let go. A dream so sweet that slumber could not conjure a better picture.

As the candle's flame wisped into smoke, Christmas Day was finally over.

And so, as both The Bennetts observed in their last sleep filled thoughts...

"God bless us, everyone."

ACKNOWLEDGEMENTS:

Thank you to my family who make me feel loved and supported every single day.

Thank you to Clarisse, the Nerds, the Soup Group, and all my friends who are the most excellent set of people.

Thank you to all the authors who inspire me every day.

Thank you to my readers for keeping me going.

Proceeds from this book sale will go to
Refuge
a Charity for women and children who have suffered domestic
violence.

Printed in Great Britain
by Amazon